HOCUS POCUS TAKES THE TRAIN

TO ADÈLE, ÉVELYNE AND LOUIS — S.D.

TO ÉLISE — R.S.

Story © 2013 Sylvie Desrosiers
Illustrations © 2013 Rémy Simard

Kids Can Press acknowledges the financial support of the Government of Ontario, through the Ontario Media Development Corporation's Ontario Book Initiative; the Ontario Arts Council; the Canada Council for the Arts; and the Government of Canada, through the CBF, for our publishing activity.

Published in Canada by
Kids Can Press Ltd.
25 Dockside Drive
Toronto, ON M5A 0B5

Published in the U.S. by
Kids Can Press Ltd.
2250 Military Road
Tonawanda, NY 14150

www.kidscanpress.com

The artwork in this book was rendered in Adobe Illustrator.

Edited by Samantha Swenson and Debbie Rogosin

CM 13 0 9 8 7 6 5 4 3 2 1

This book is smyth sewn casebound.
Manufactured in Shenzhen, China, in 3/2013 through Asia Pacific Offset

Library and Archives Canada Cataloguing in Publication

Desrosiers, Sylvie, 1954–
    Hocus pocus takes the train / written by Sylvie Desrosiers;
illustrated by Rémy Simard.

(Hocus Pocus)
ISBN 978-1-55453-956-7

I. Simard, Rémy II. Title.

PS8557.E8745H64 2013   jC813'.54   C2012-907764-X

Kids Can Press is a Corus™ Entertainment company

HOCUS POCUS
TAKES THE TRAIN

SYLVIE DESROSIERS

RÉMY SIMARD

KIDS CAN PRESS

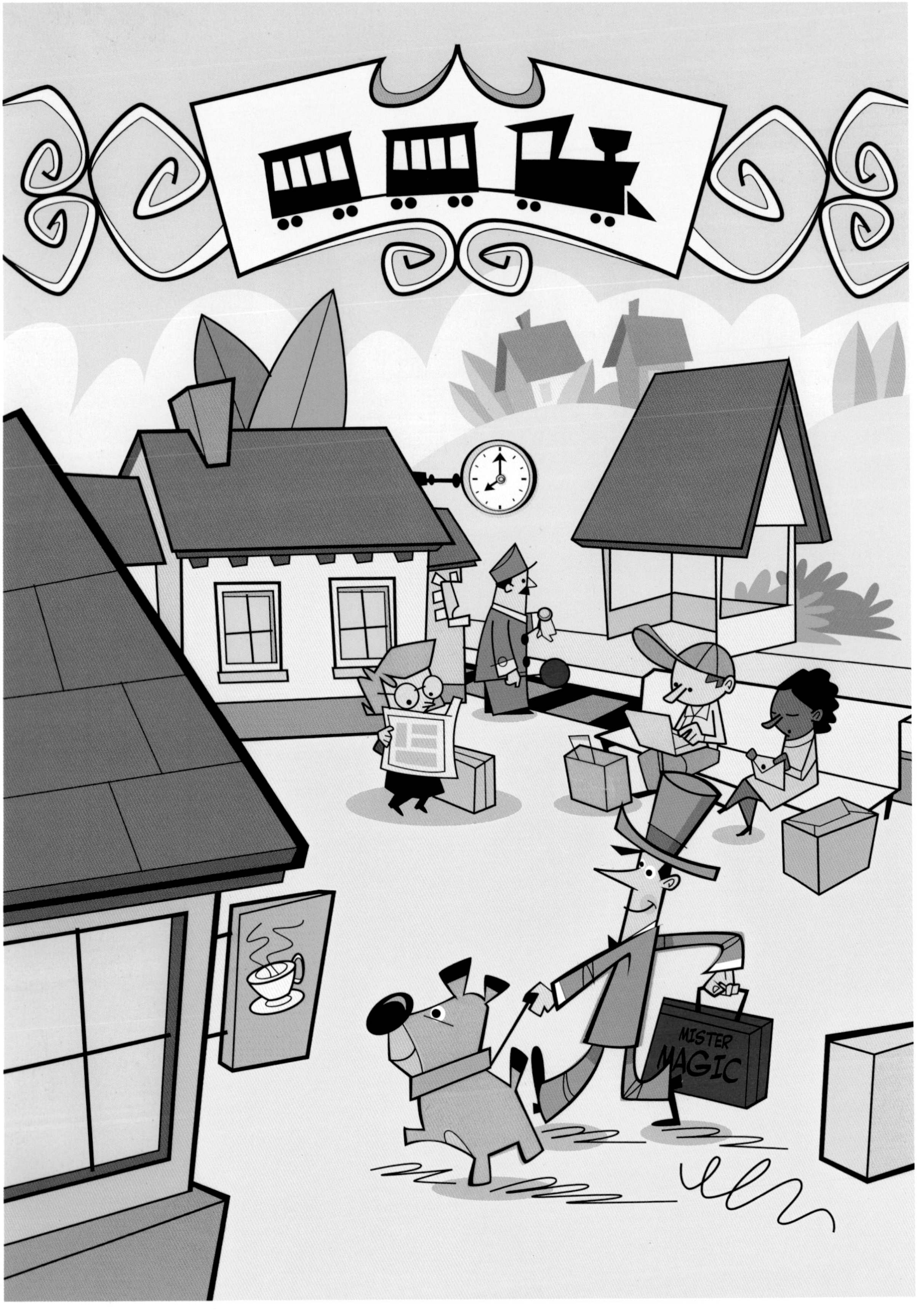
MISTER
MAGIC

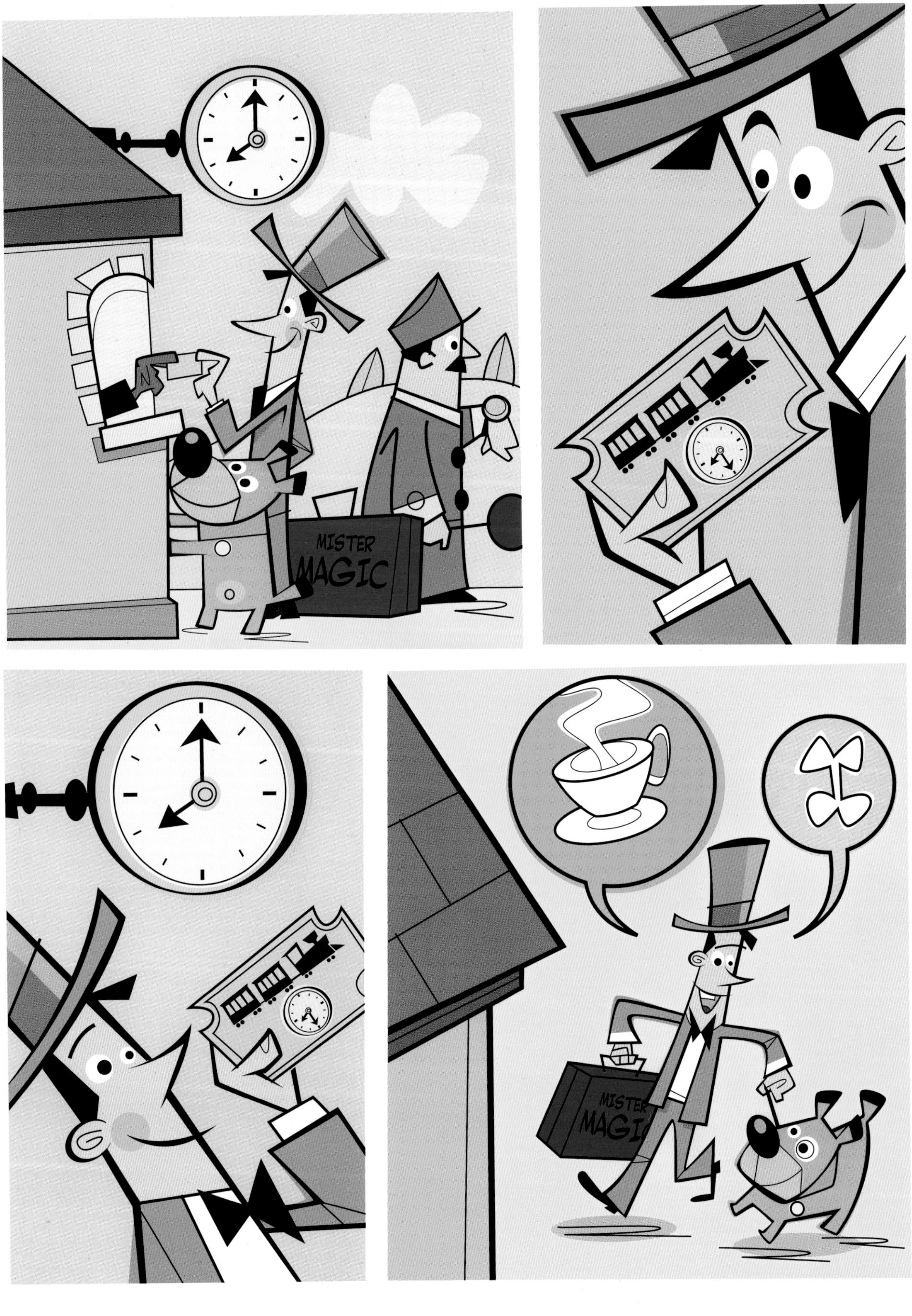
MISTER
MAGIC

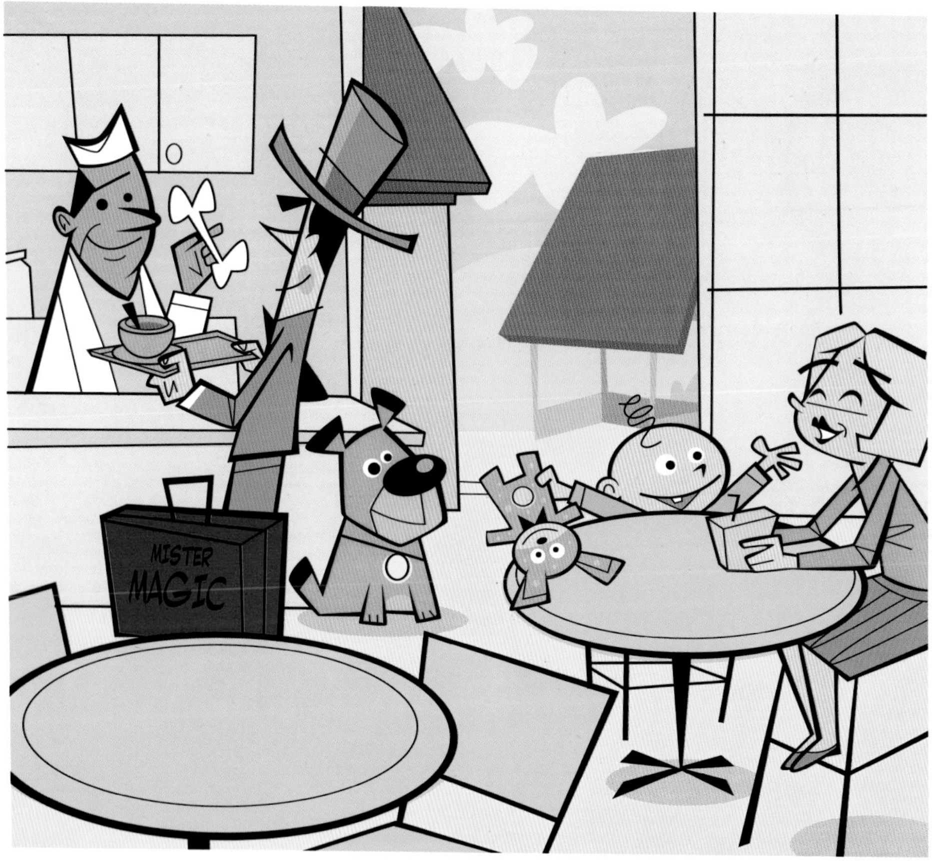
MISTER
MAGIC

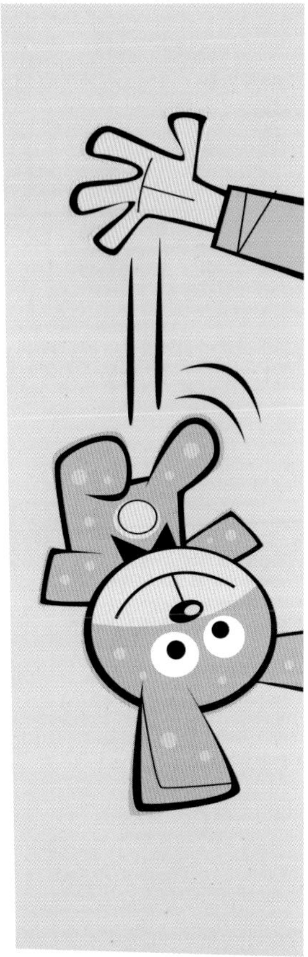

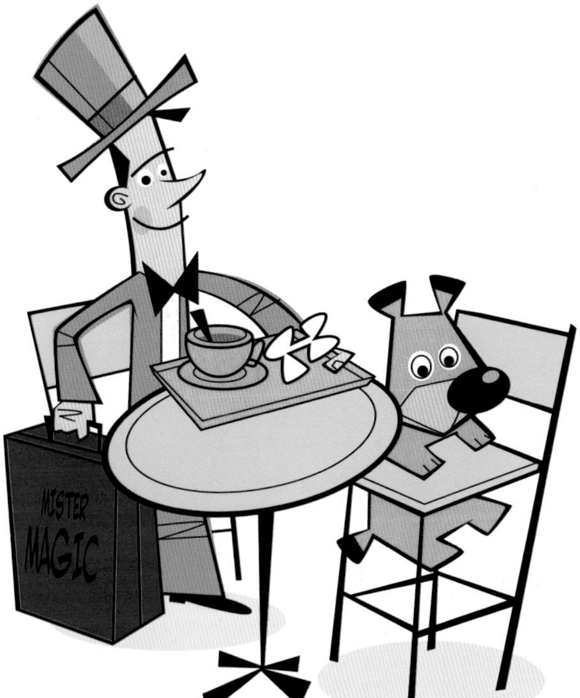
MISTER
MAGIC

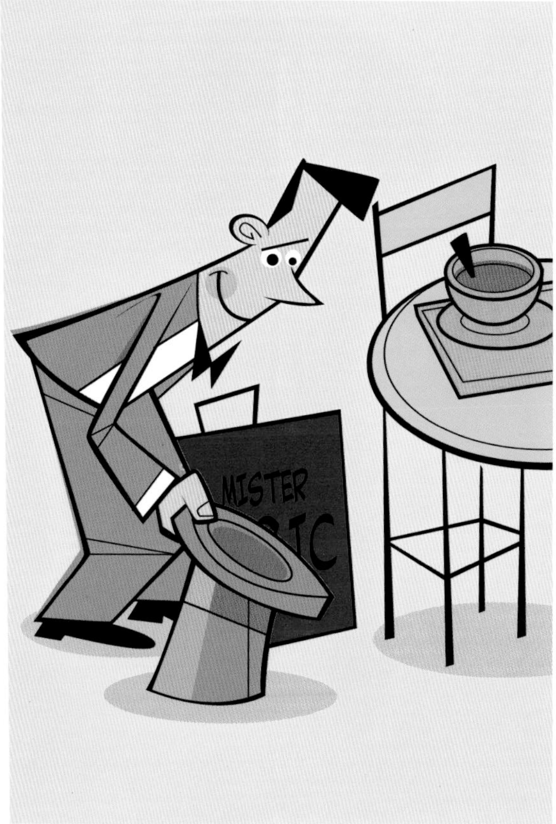
MISTER

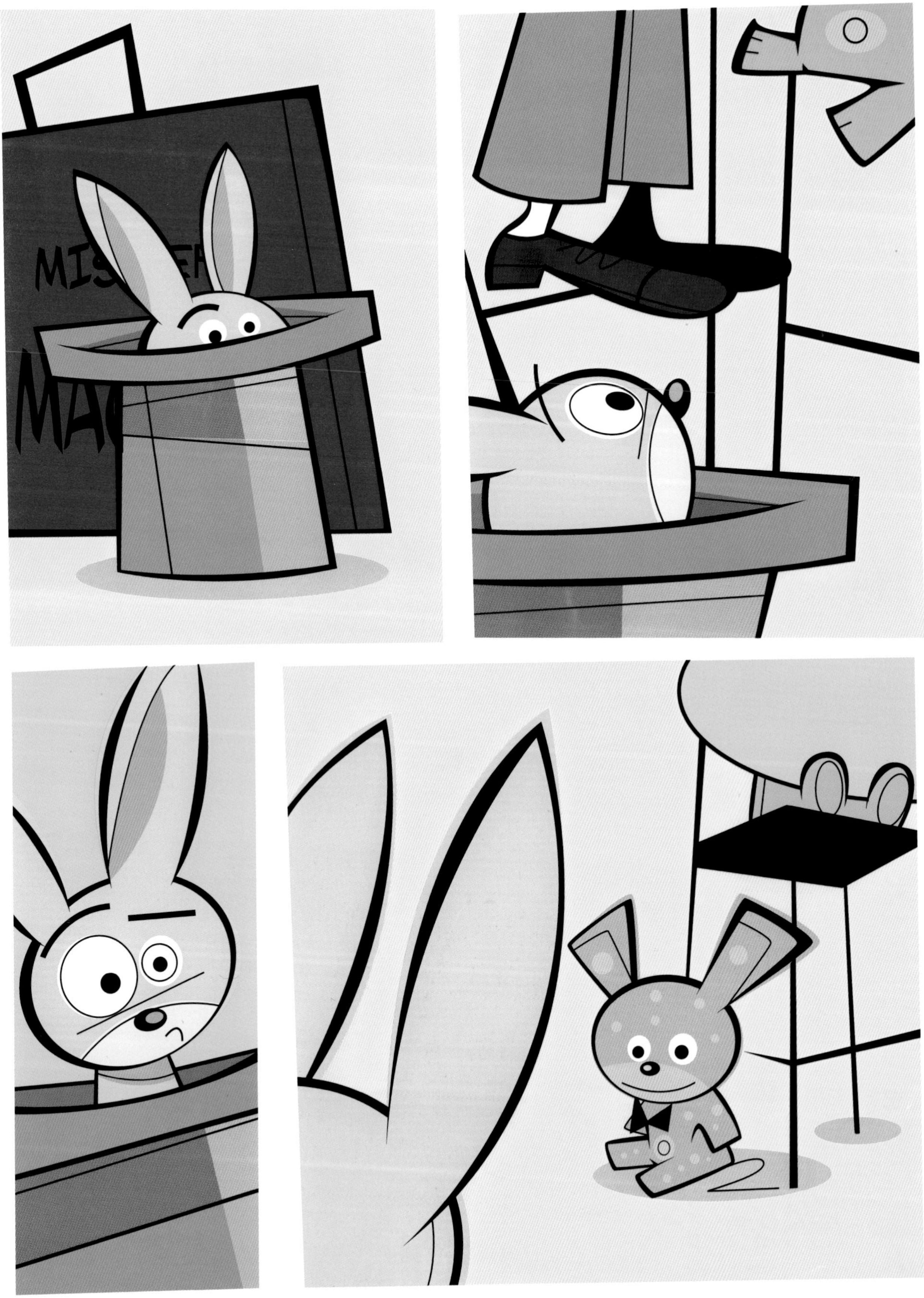

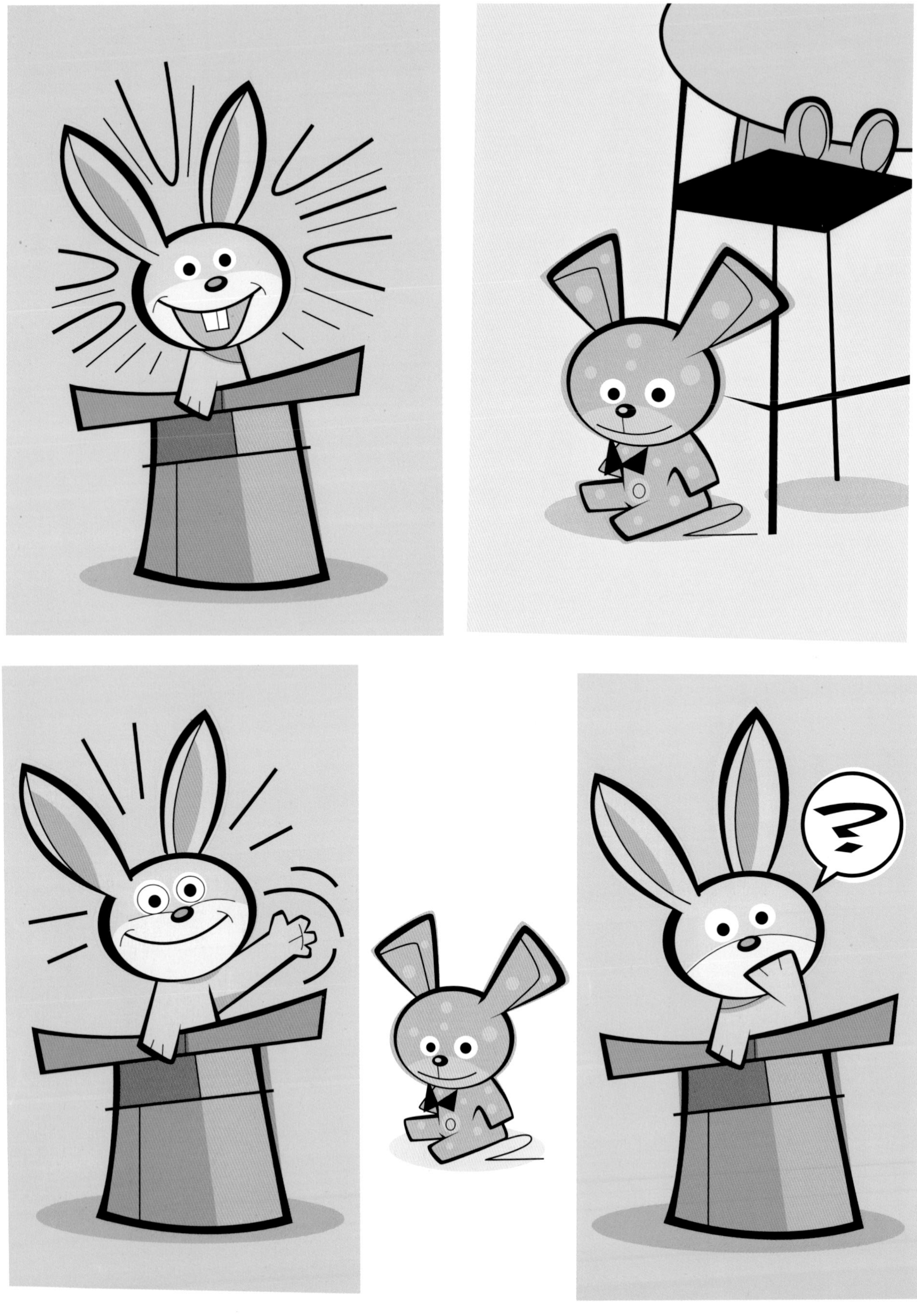

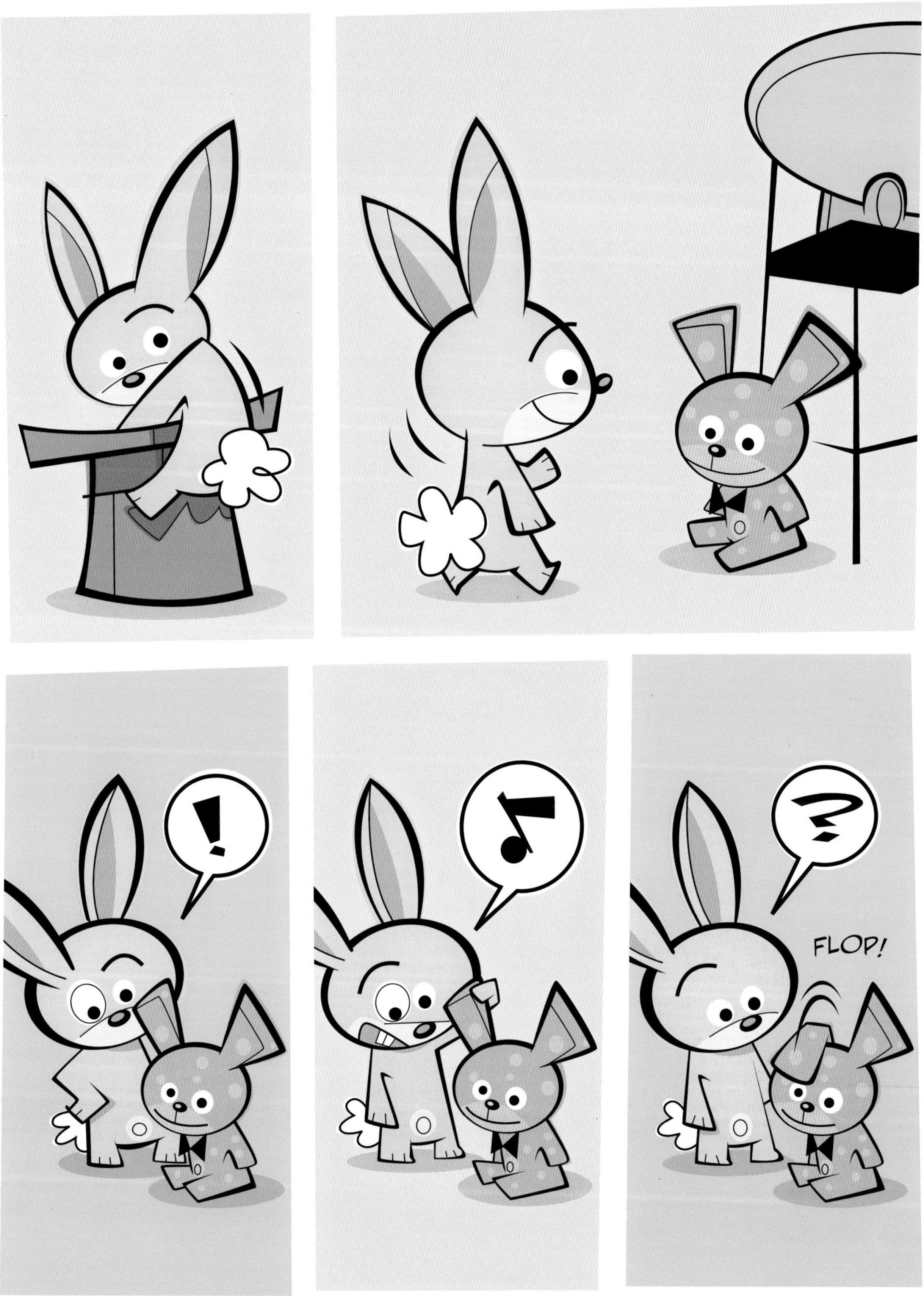
!
FLOP!

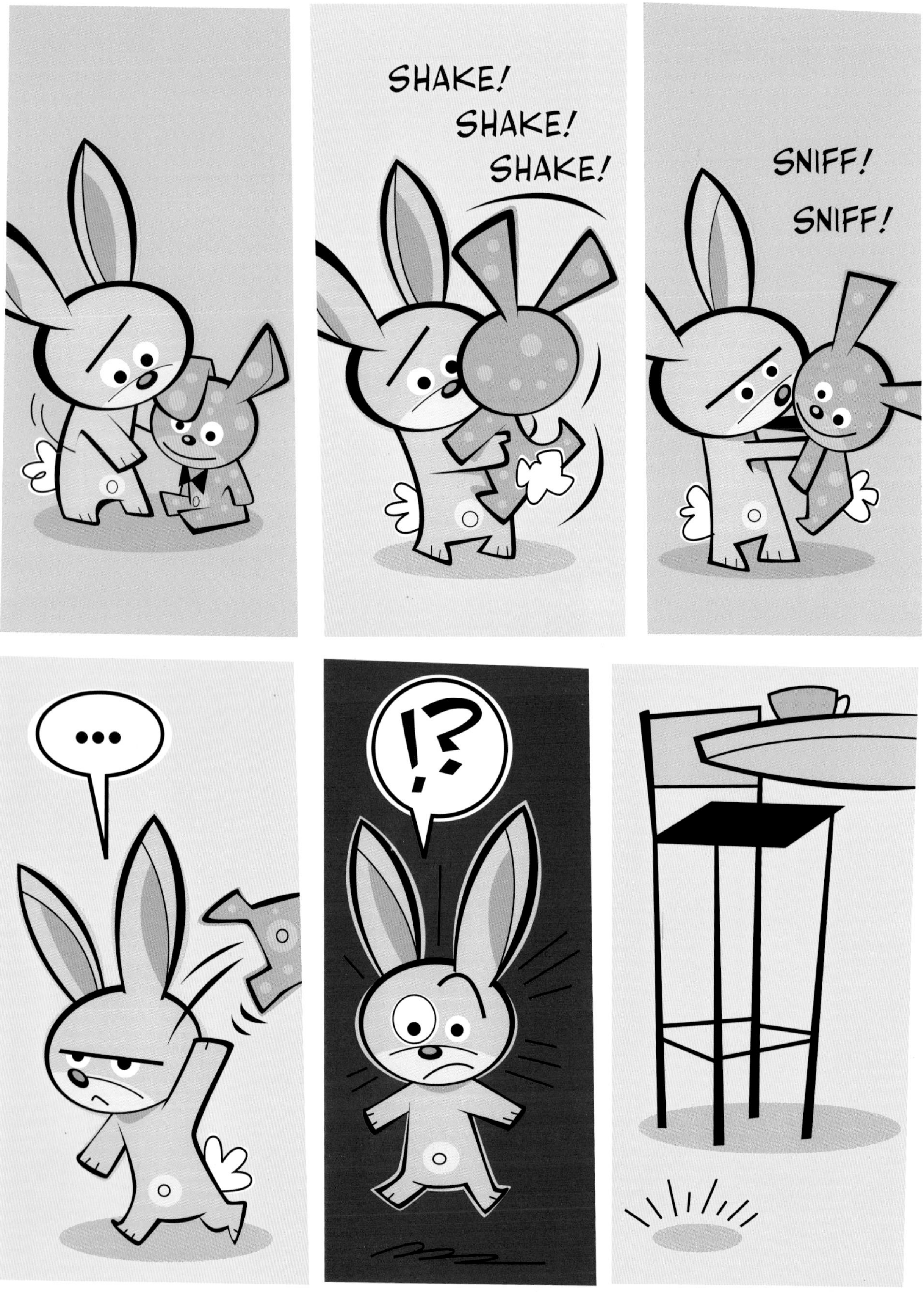
SHAKE!
SHAKE!
SHAKE!
SNIFF!
SNIFF!
...
!?

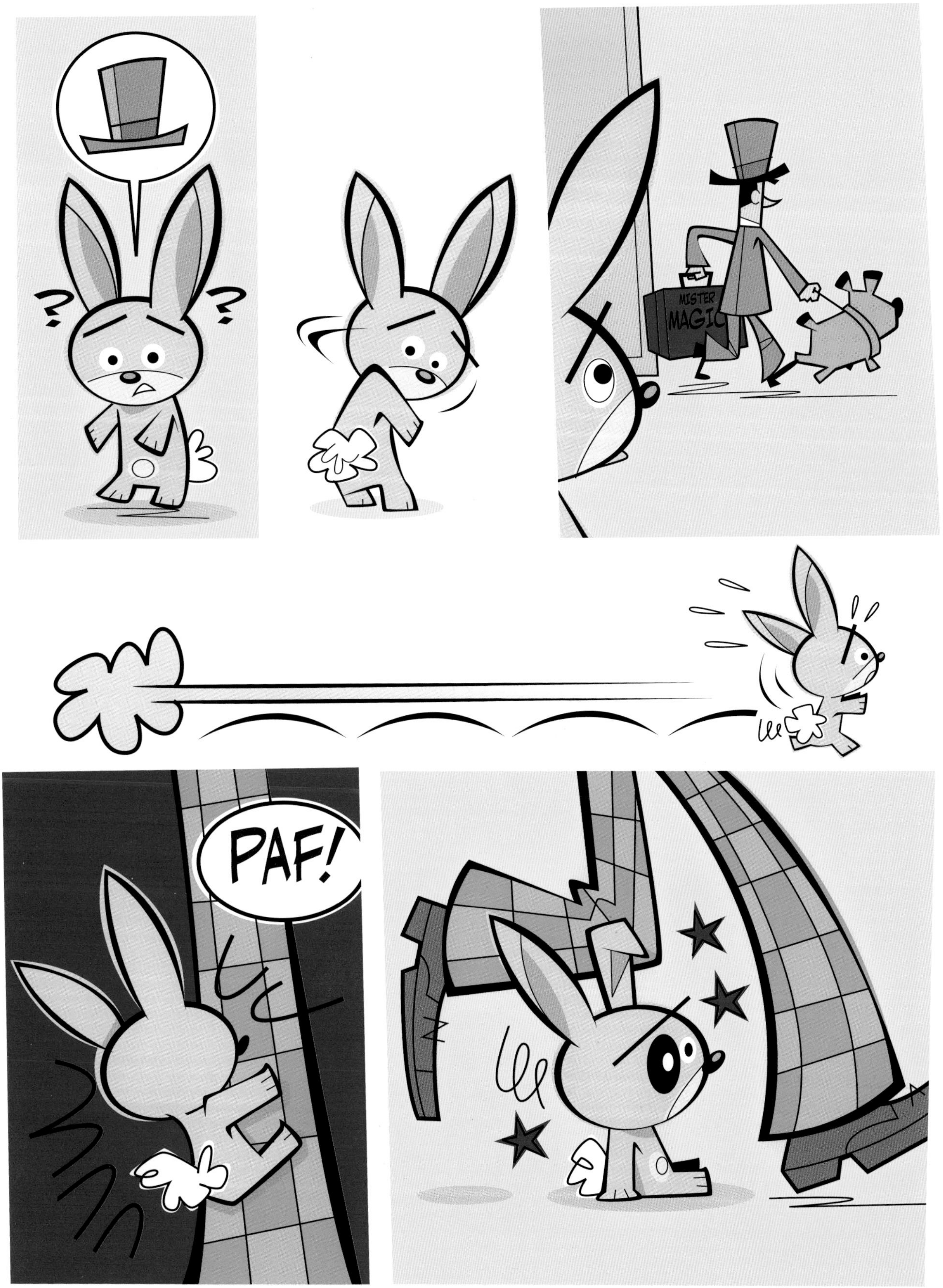
MISTER
MAGIC
PAF!

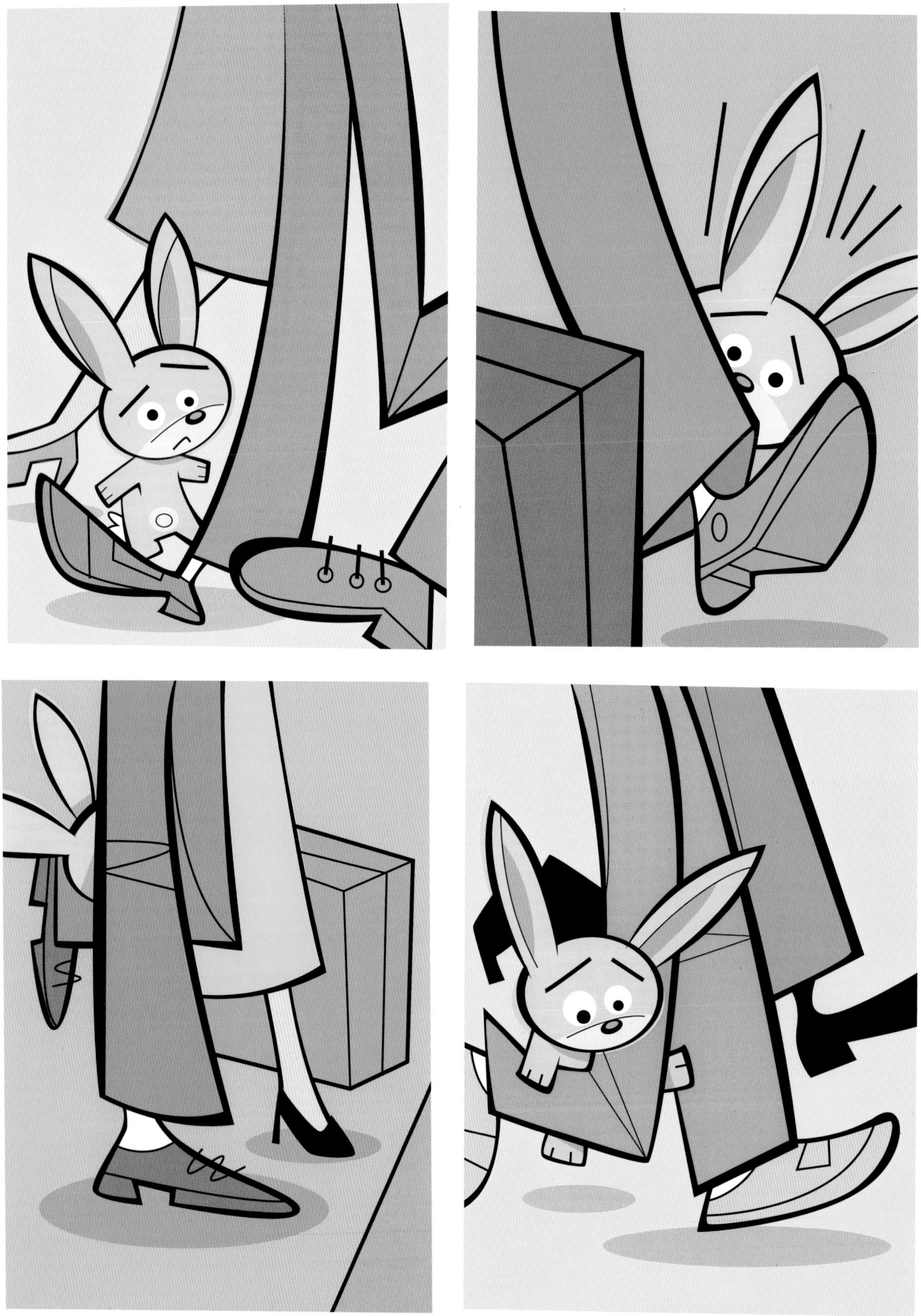

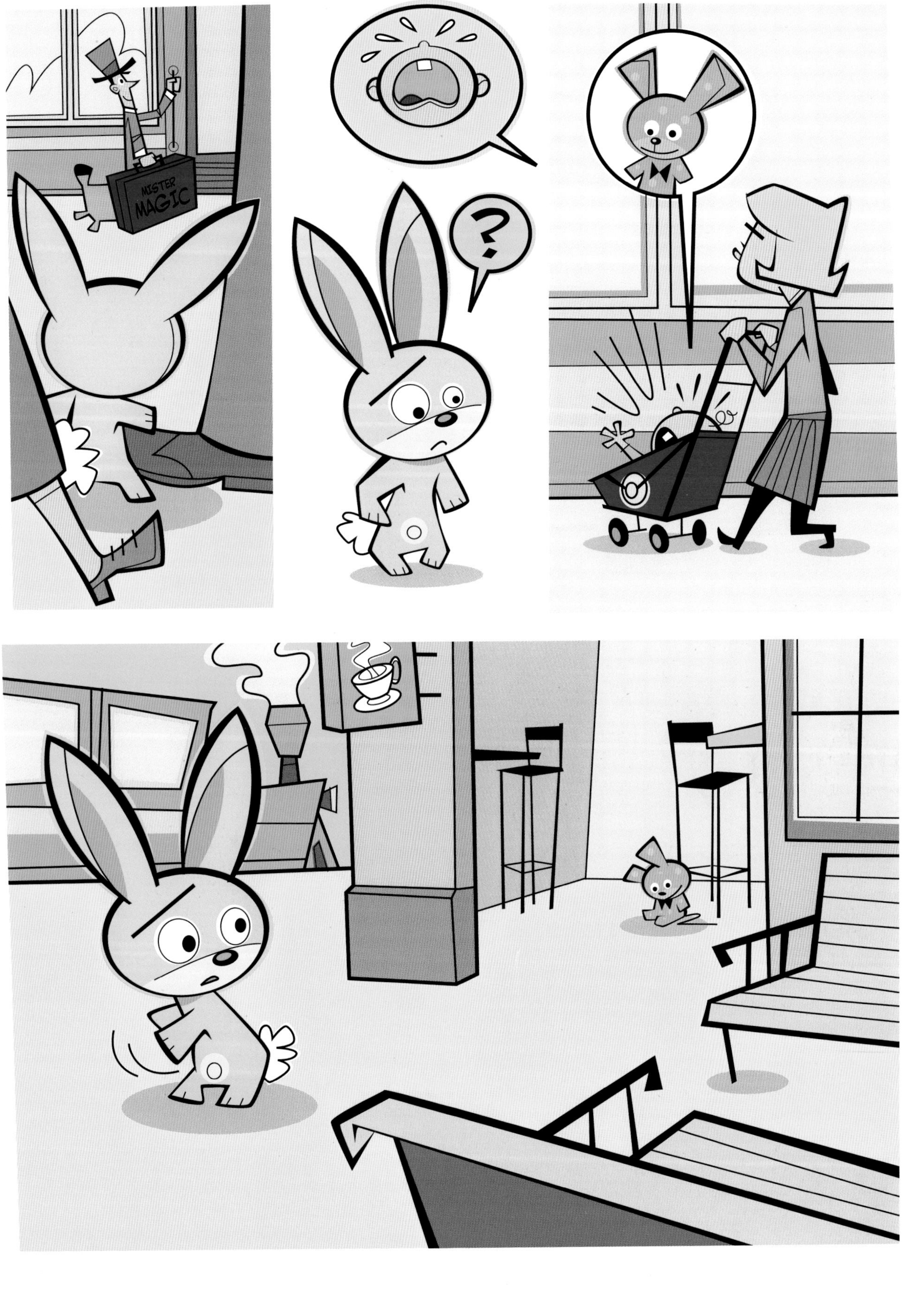
MISTER
MAGIC
?

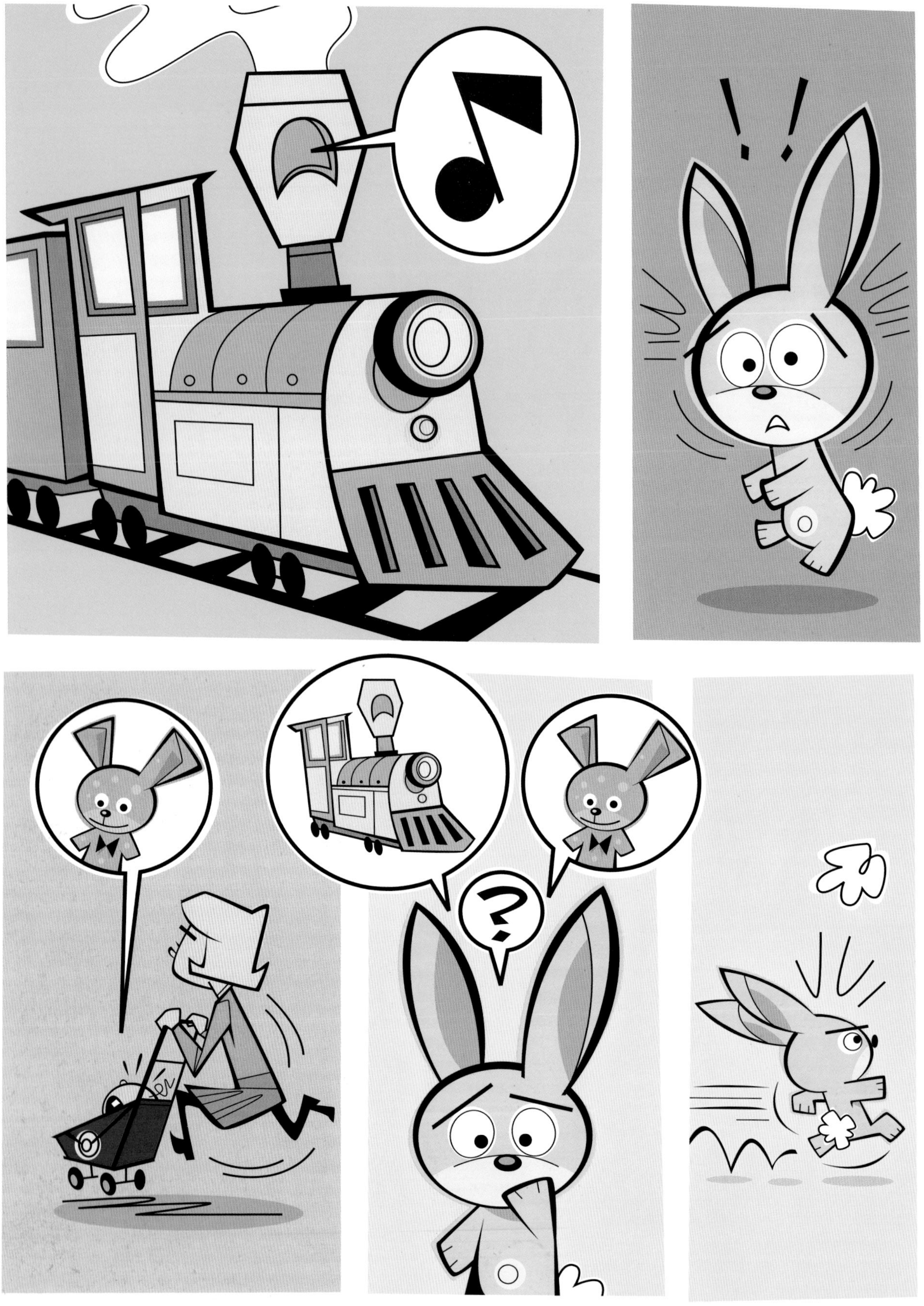

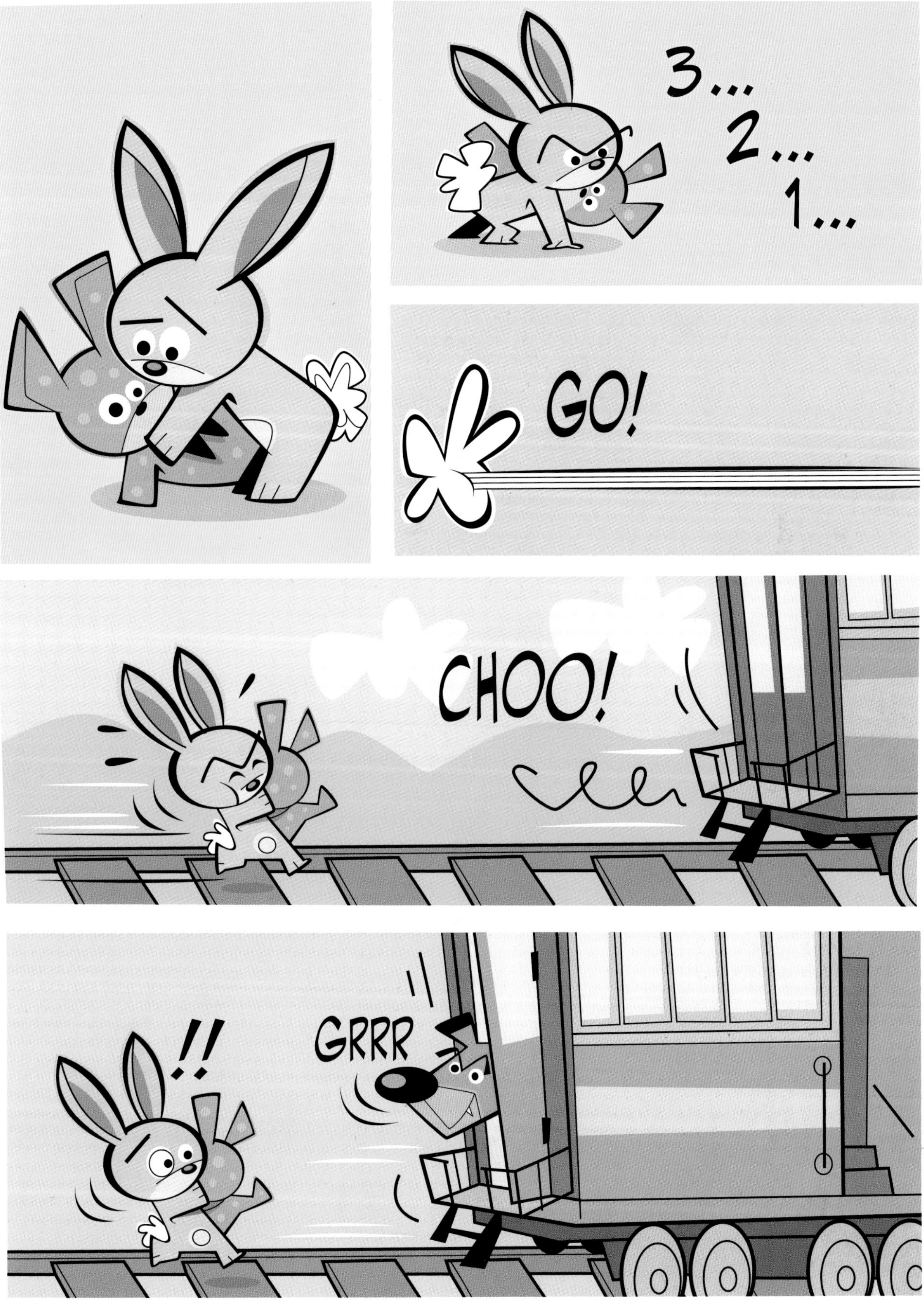
3...
2...
1...
GO!
CHOO!
!!
GRRR

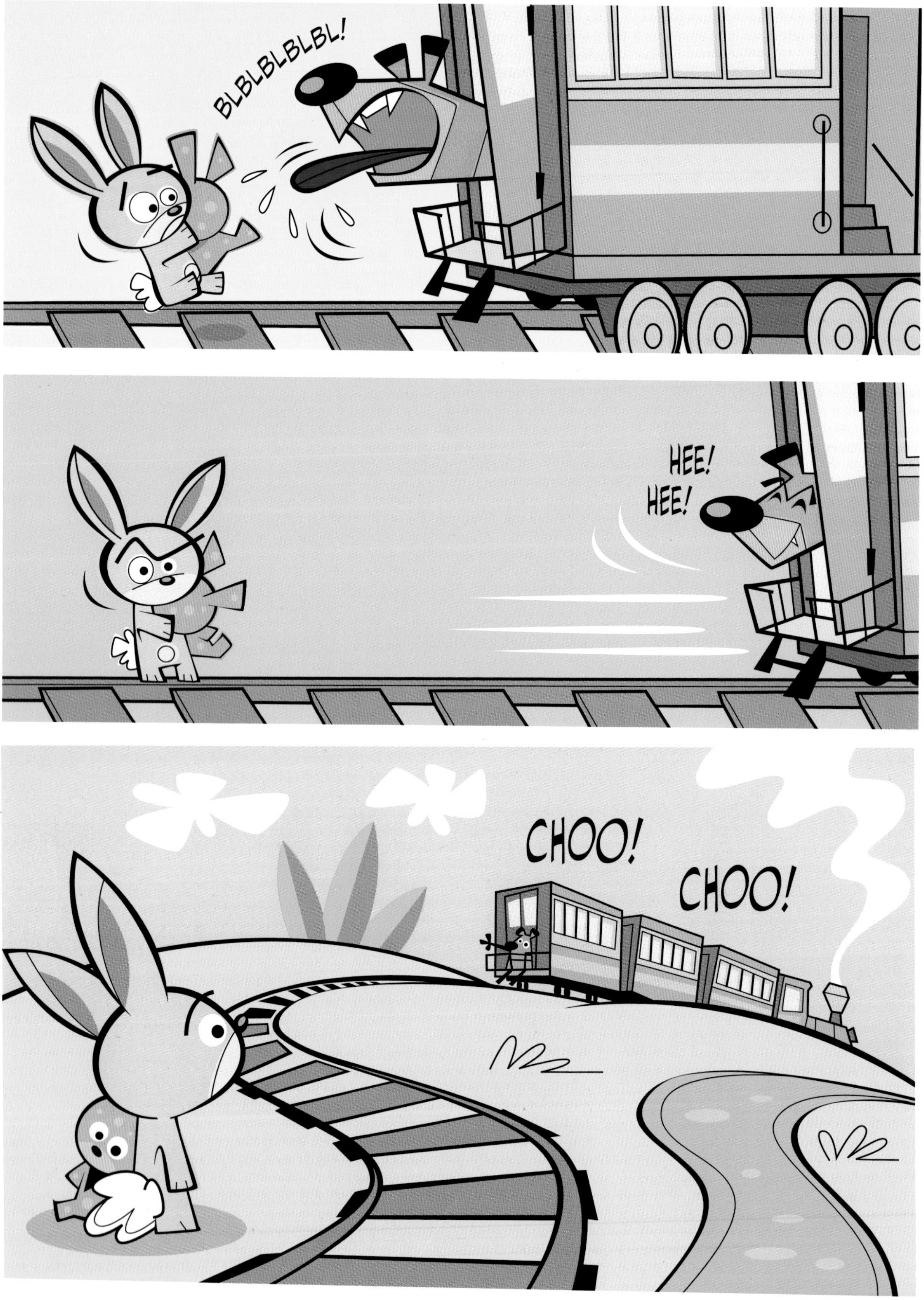
BLBLBLBLBL!
HEE!
HEE!
CHOO!
CHOO!

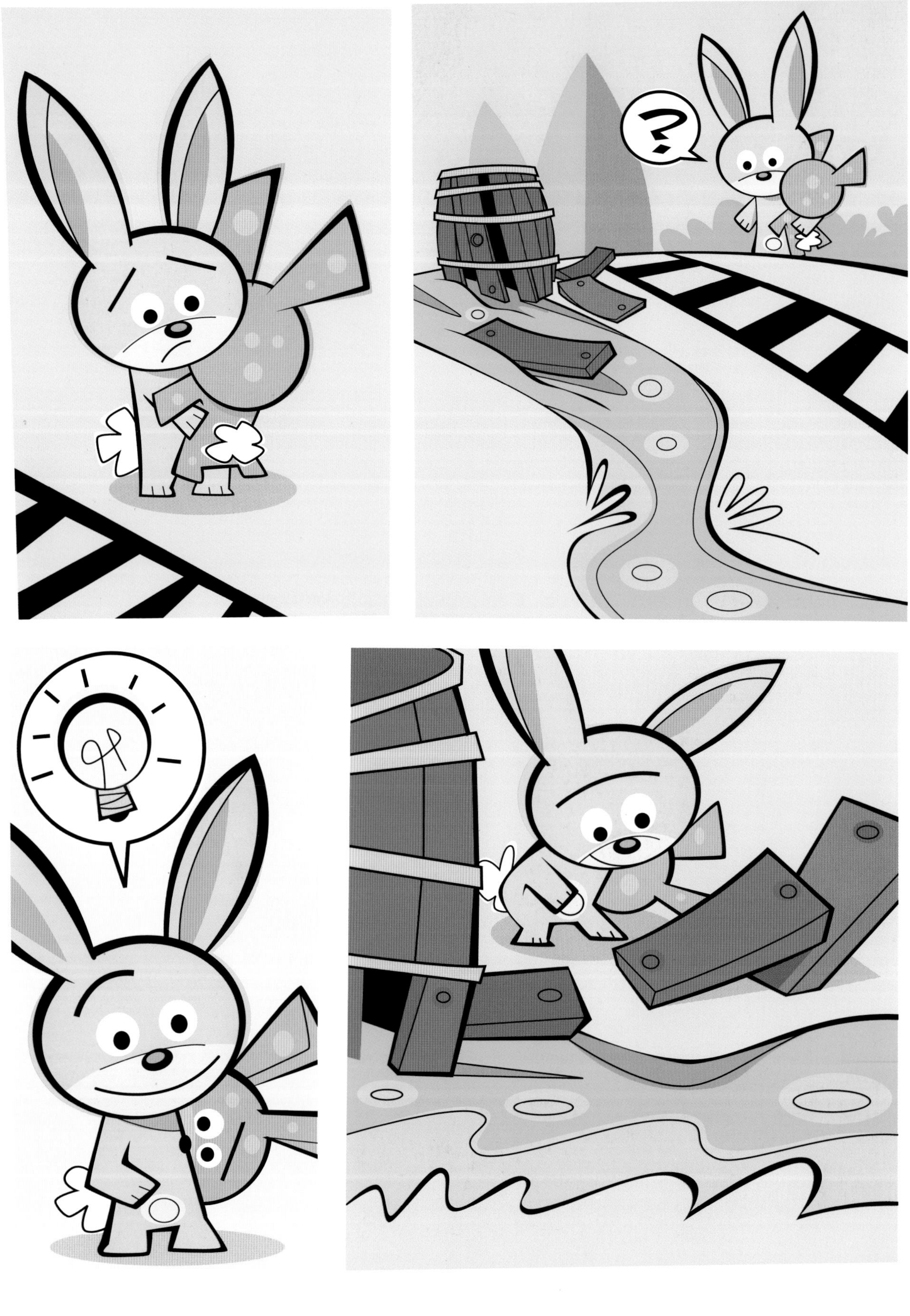
?

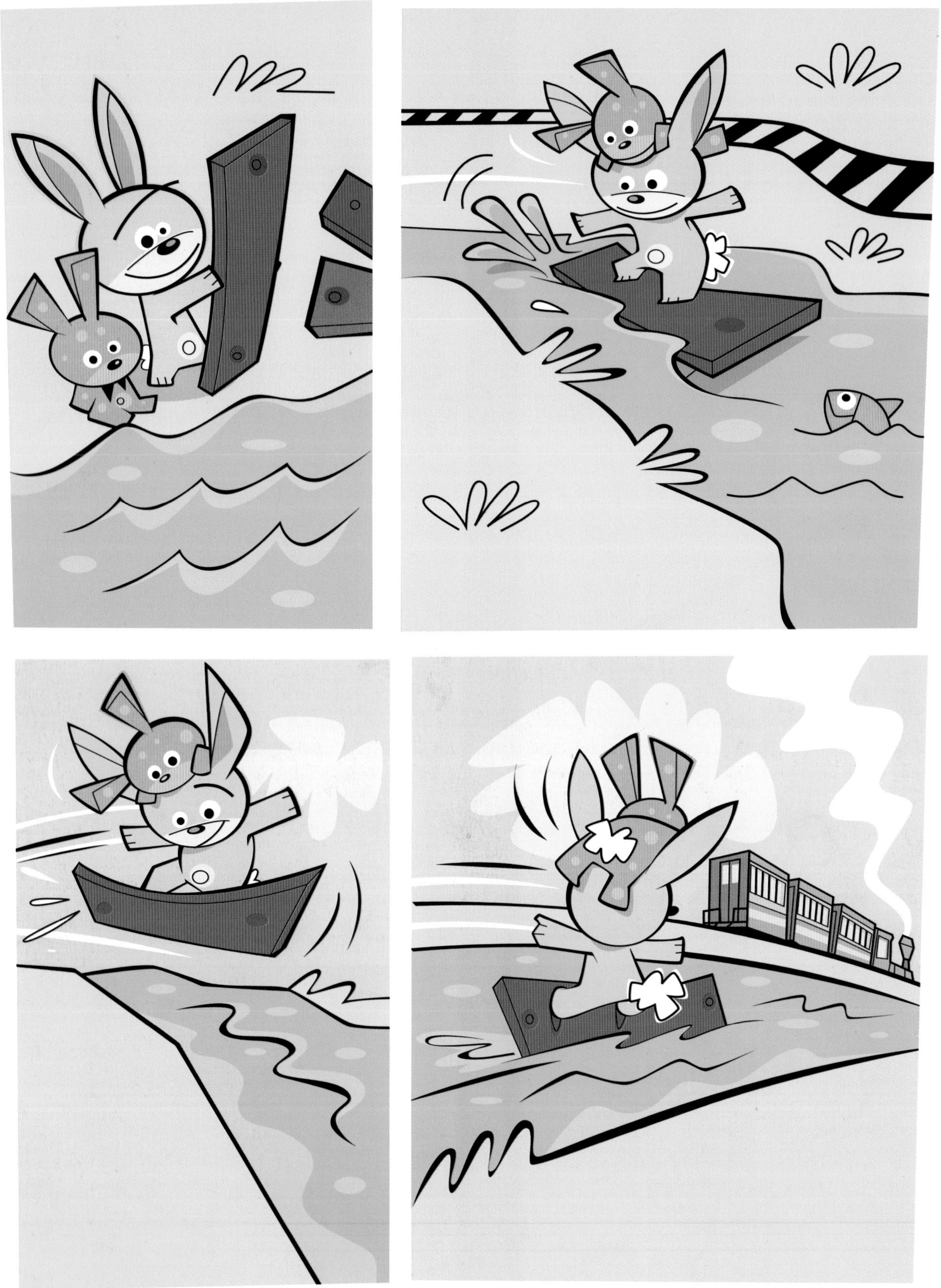

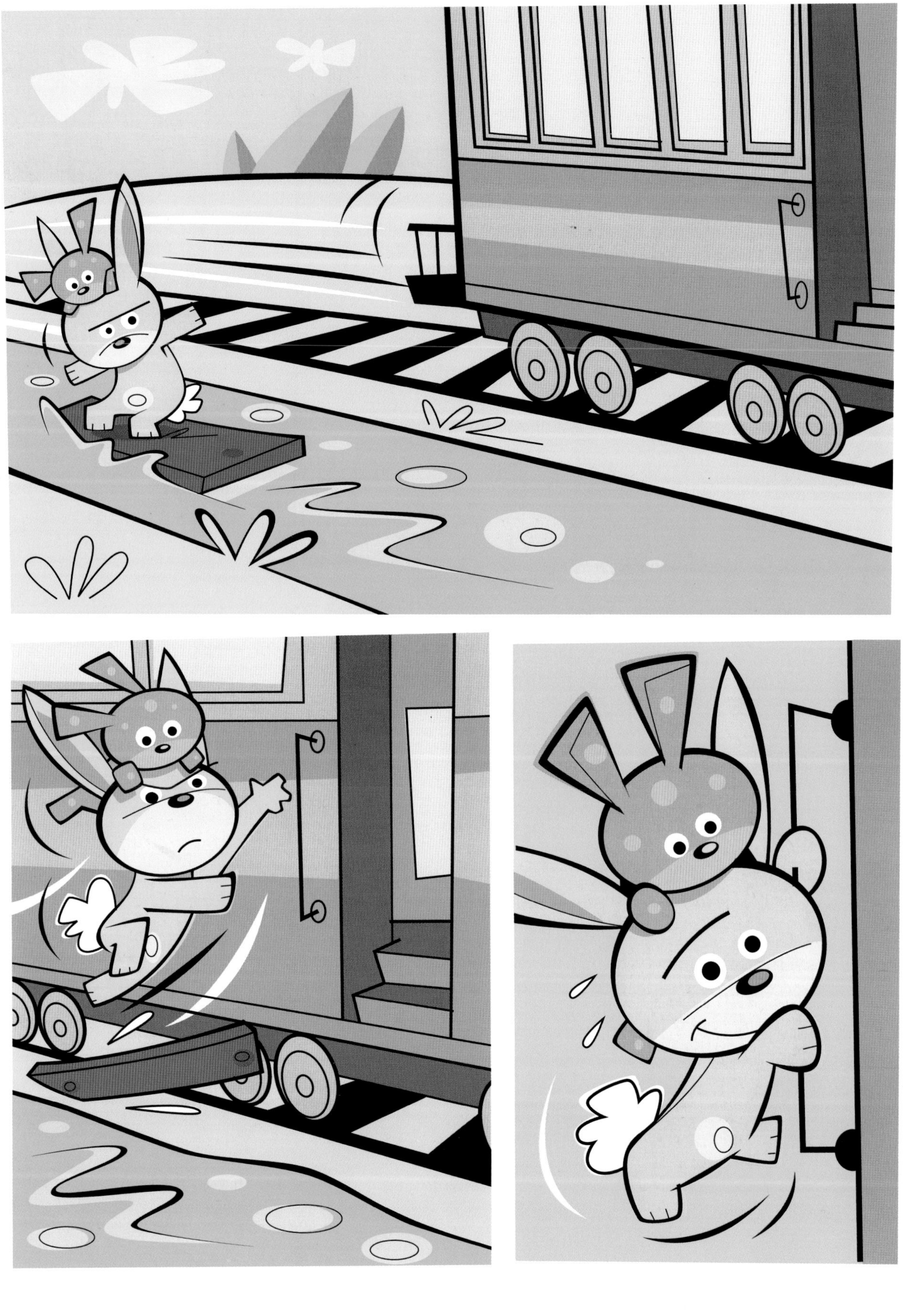

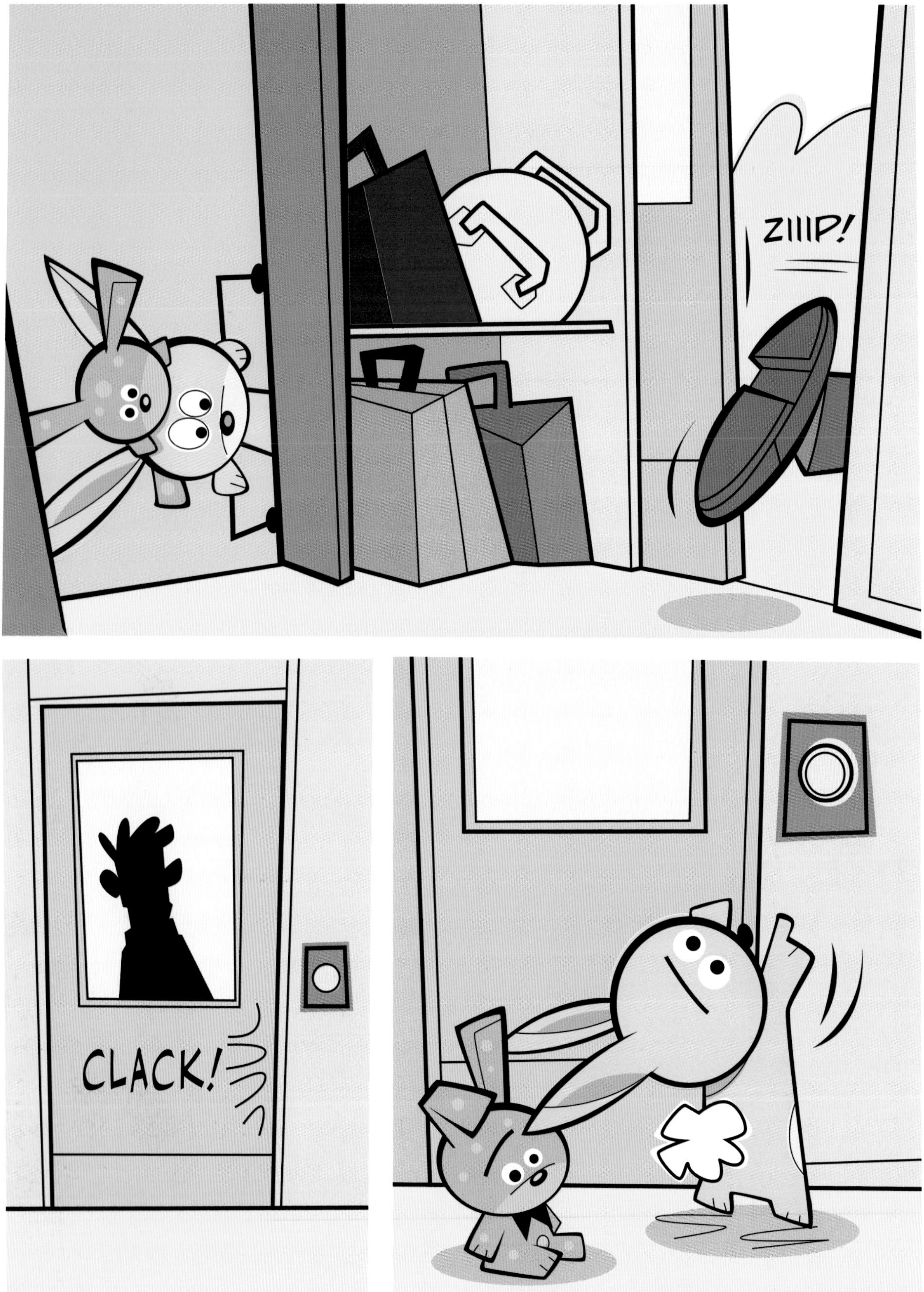

ZIIIP!
CLACK!

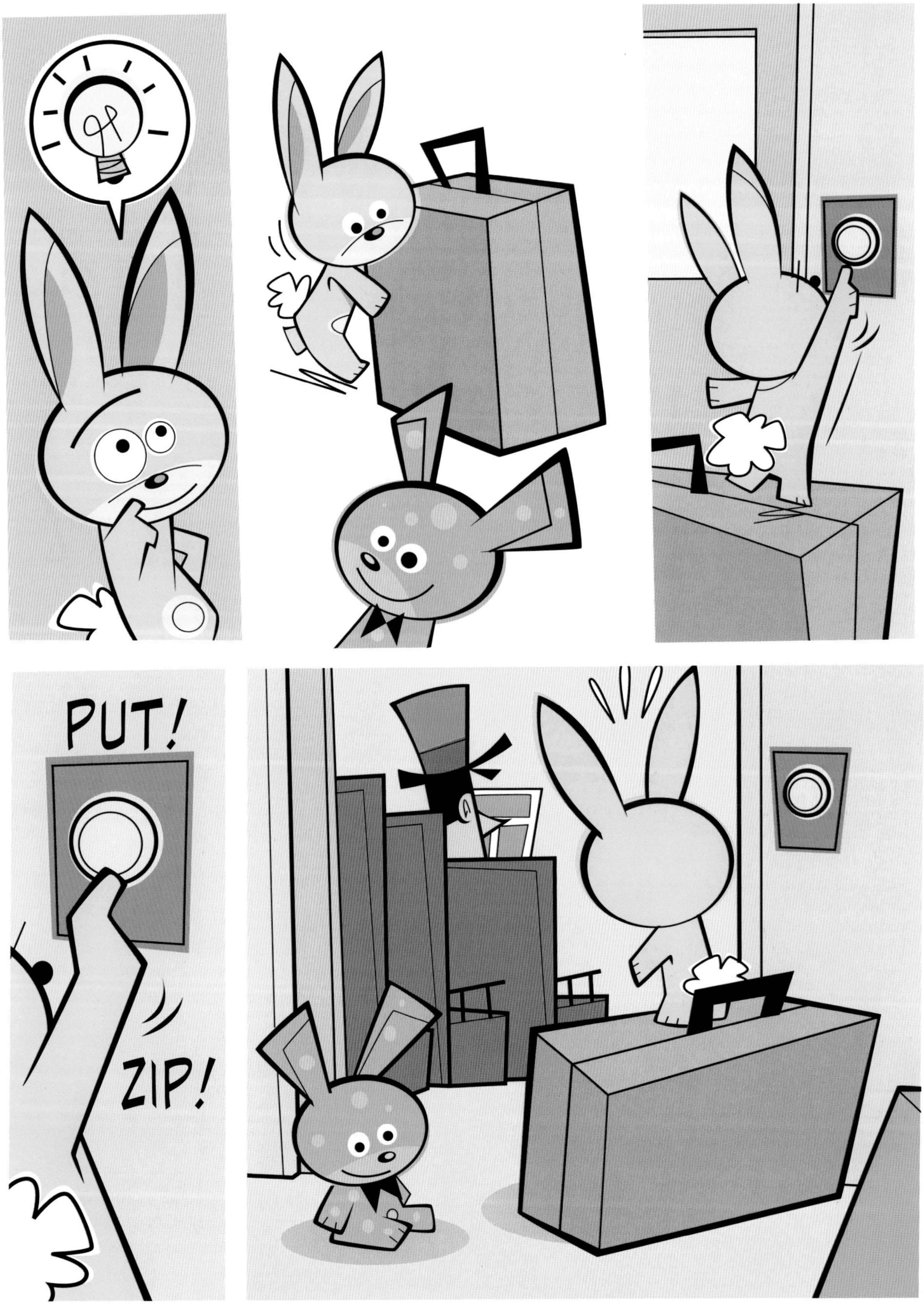
PUT!
ZIP!

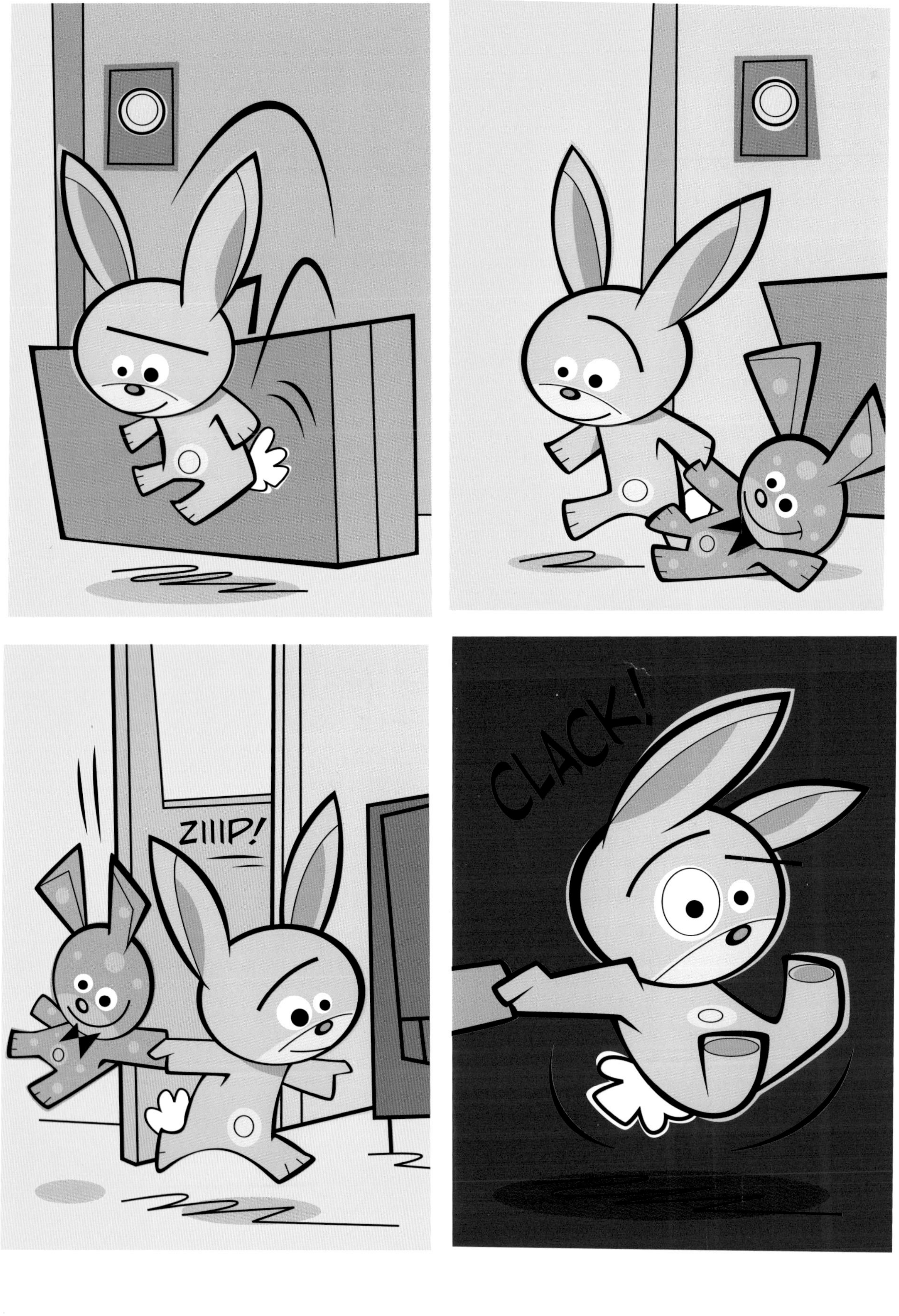
ZIIIP!
CLACK!

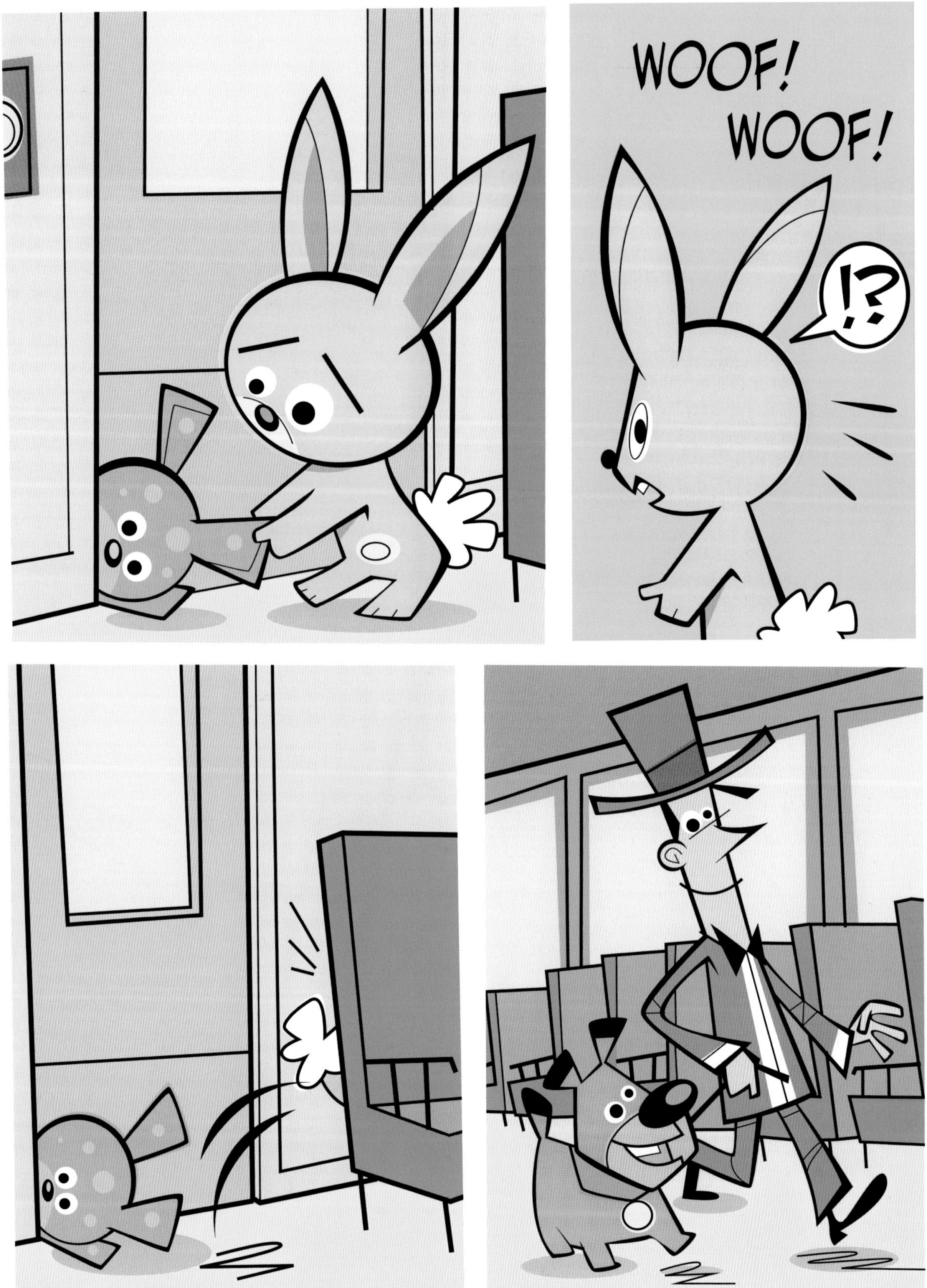
WOOF!
WOOF!
!?

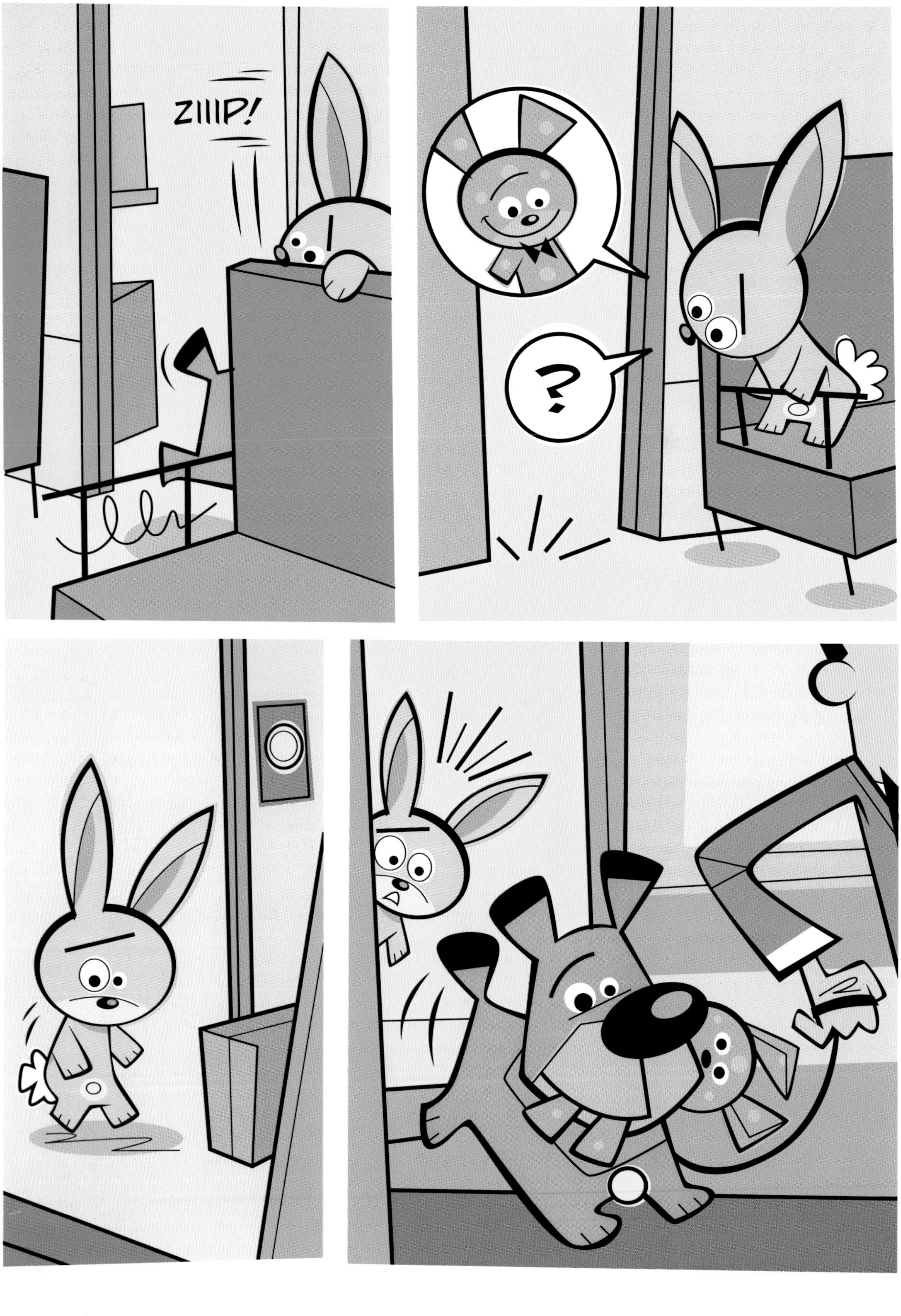
ZIIIP!
?

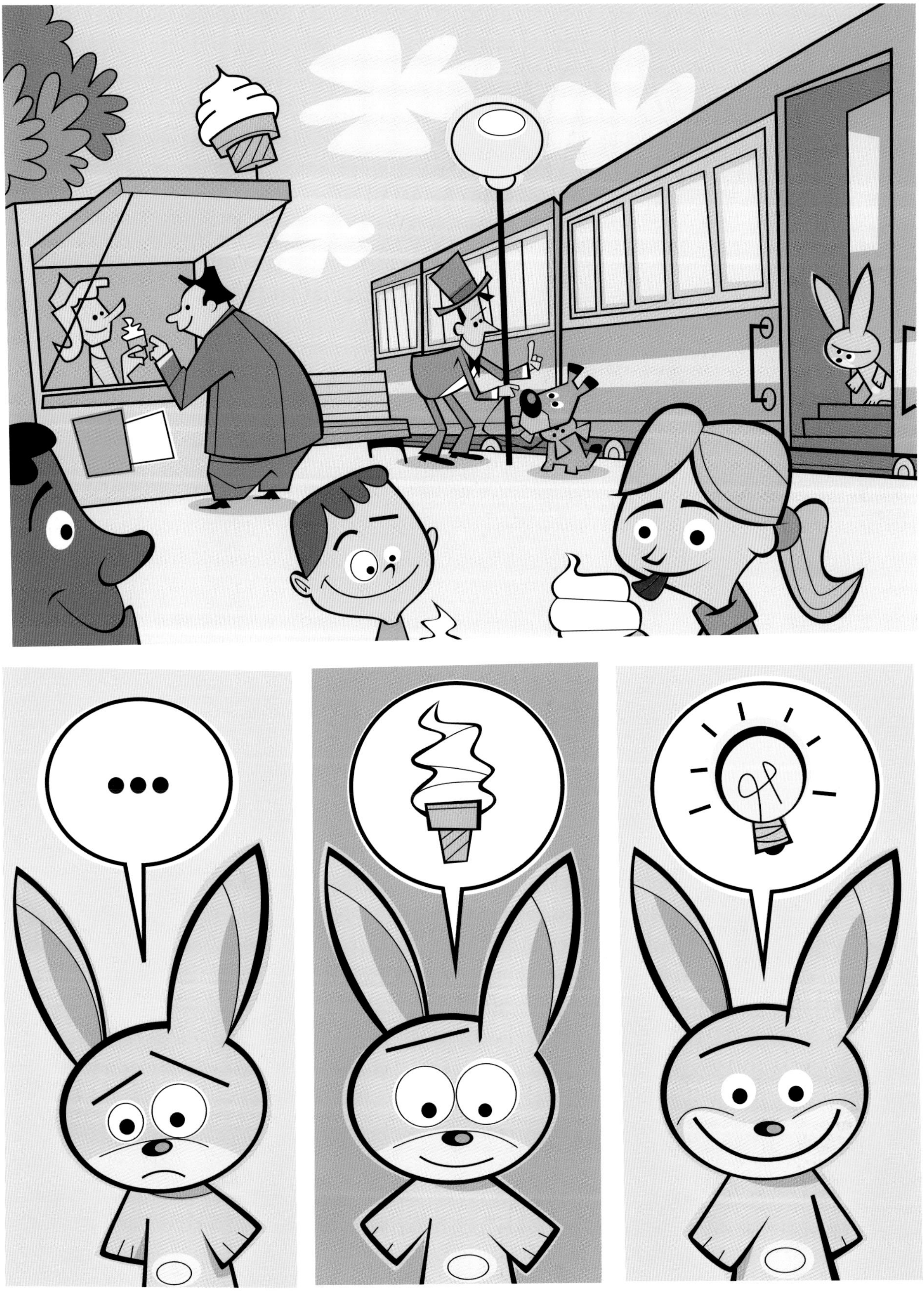

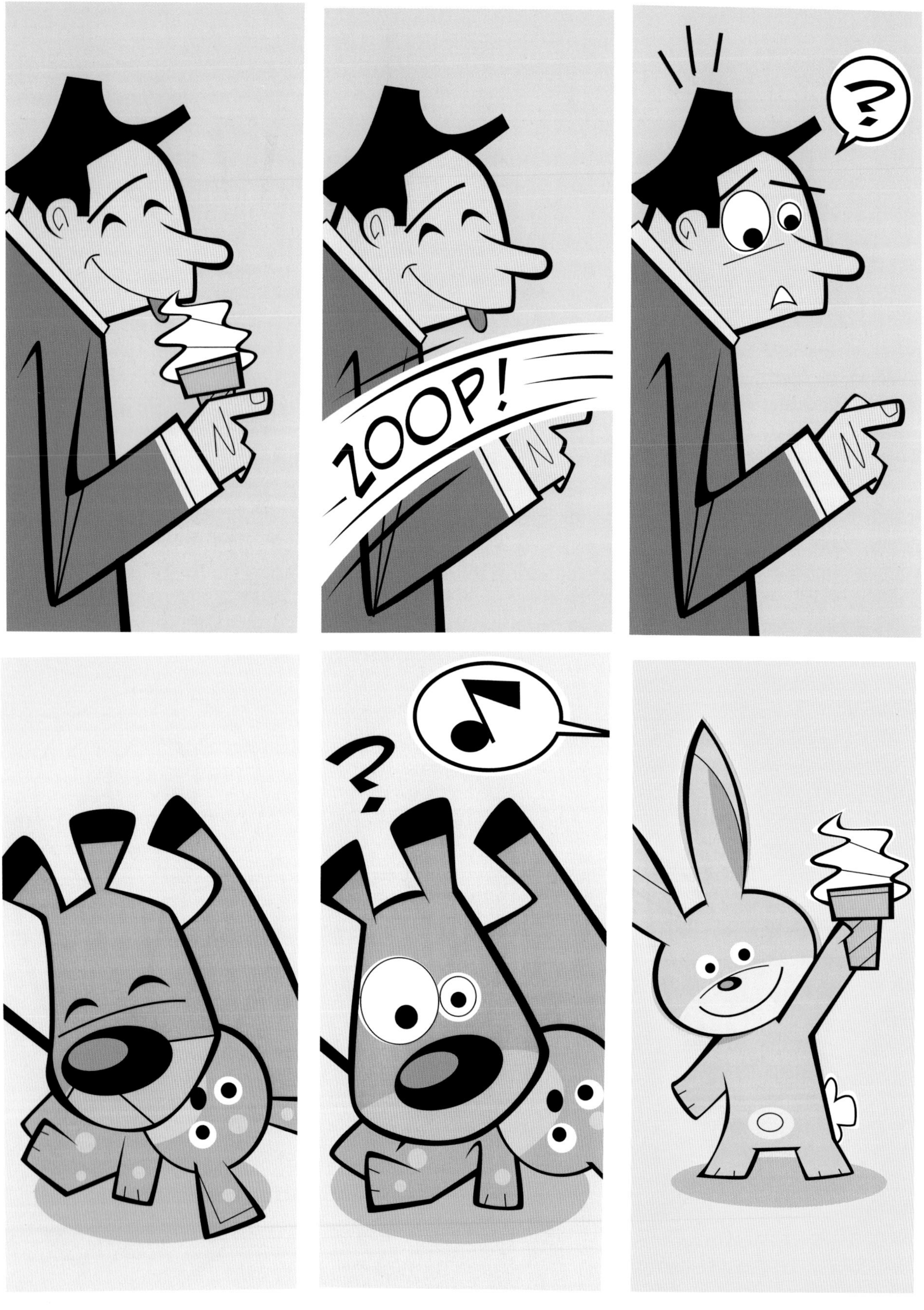
ZOOP!

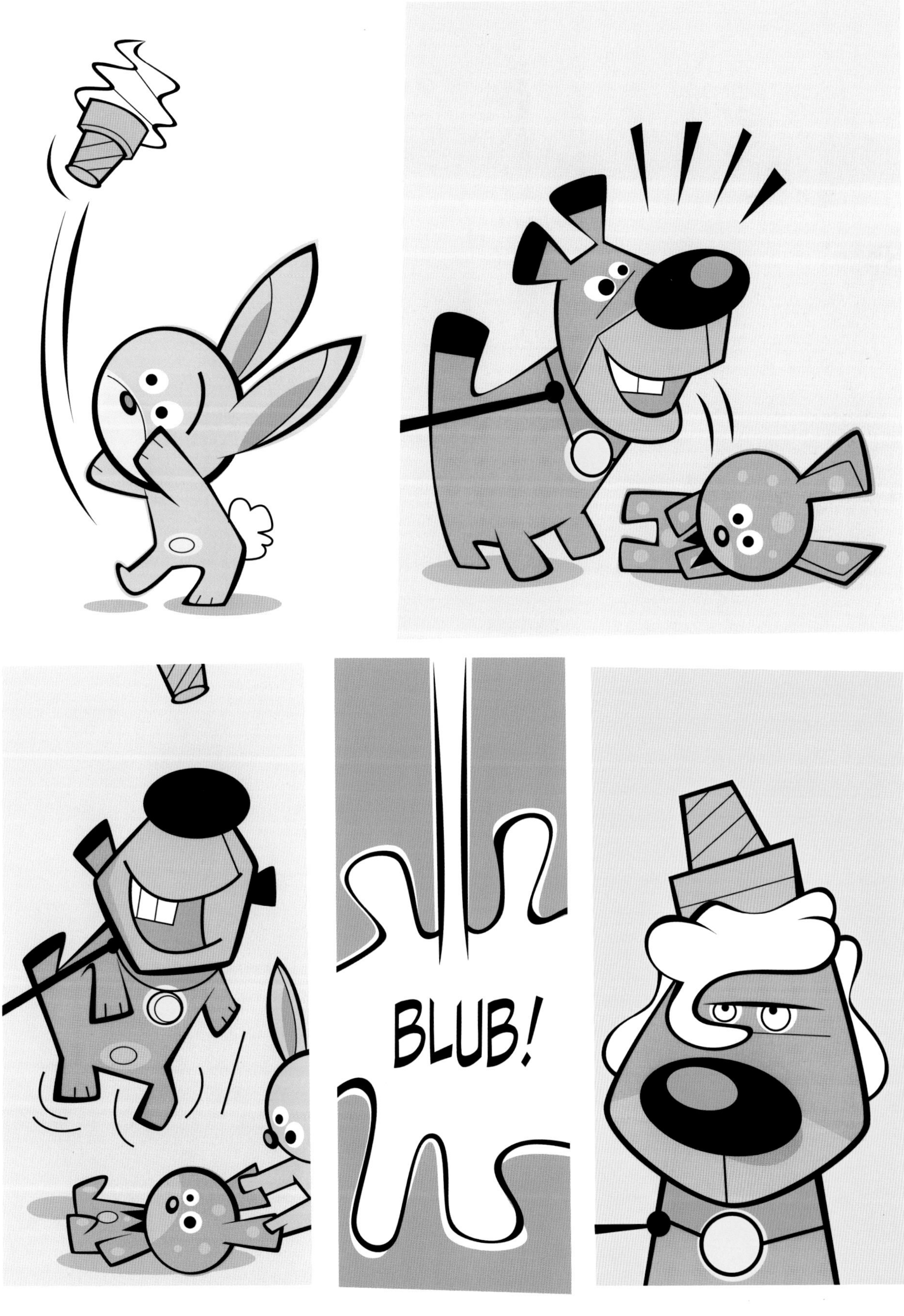
BLUB!

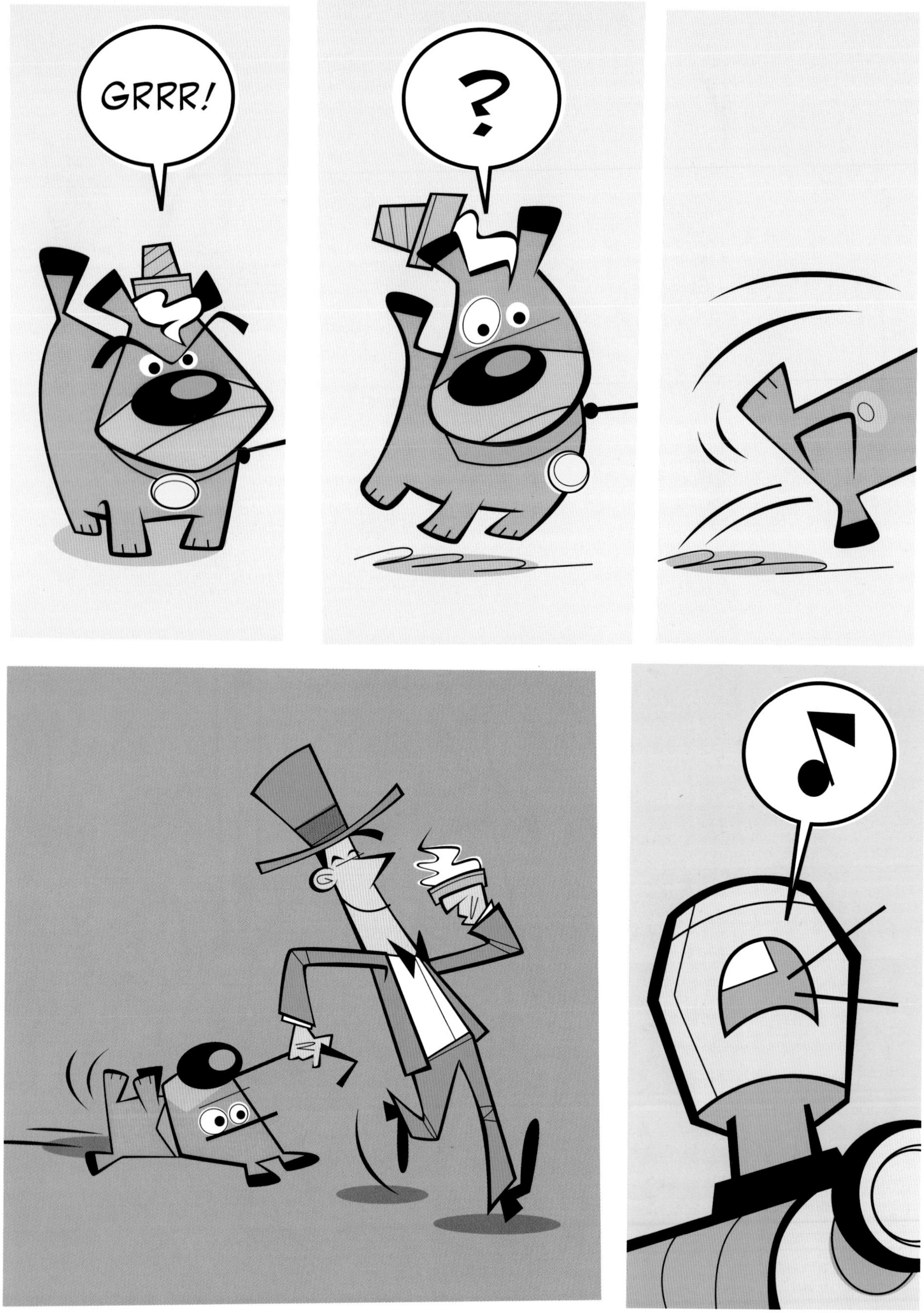
GRRR!
?

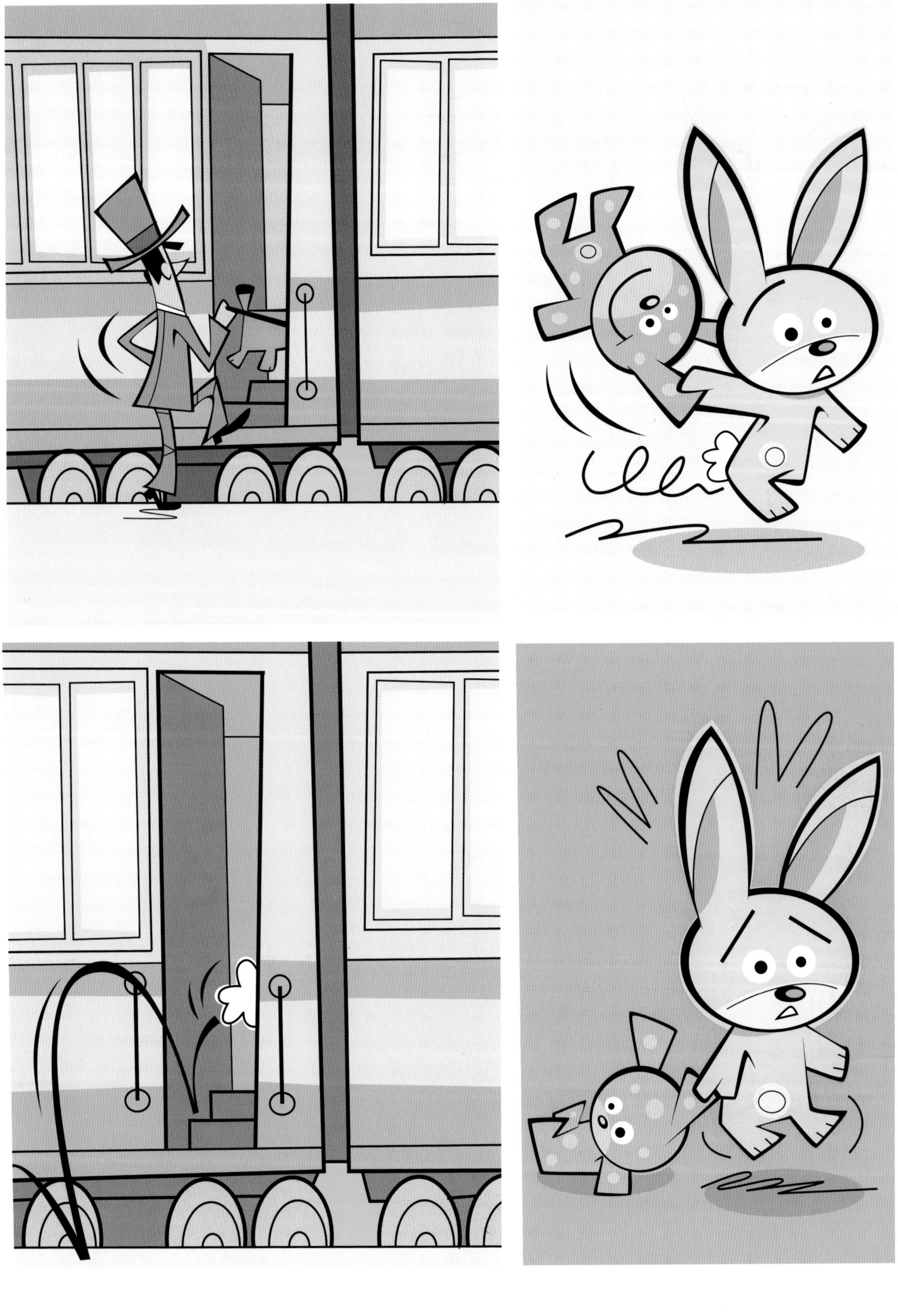

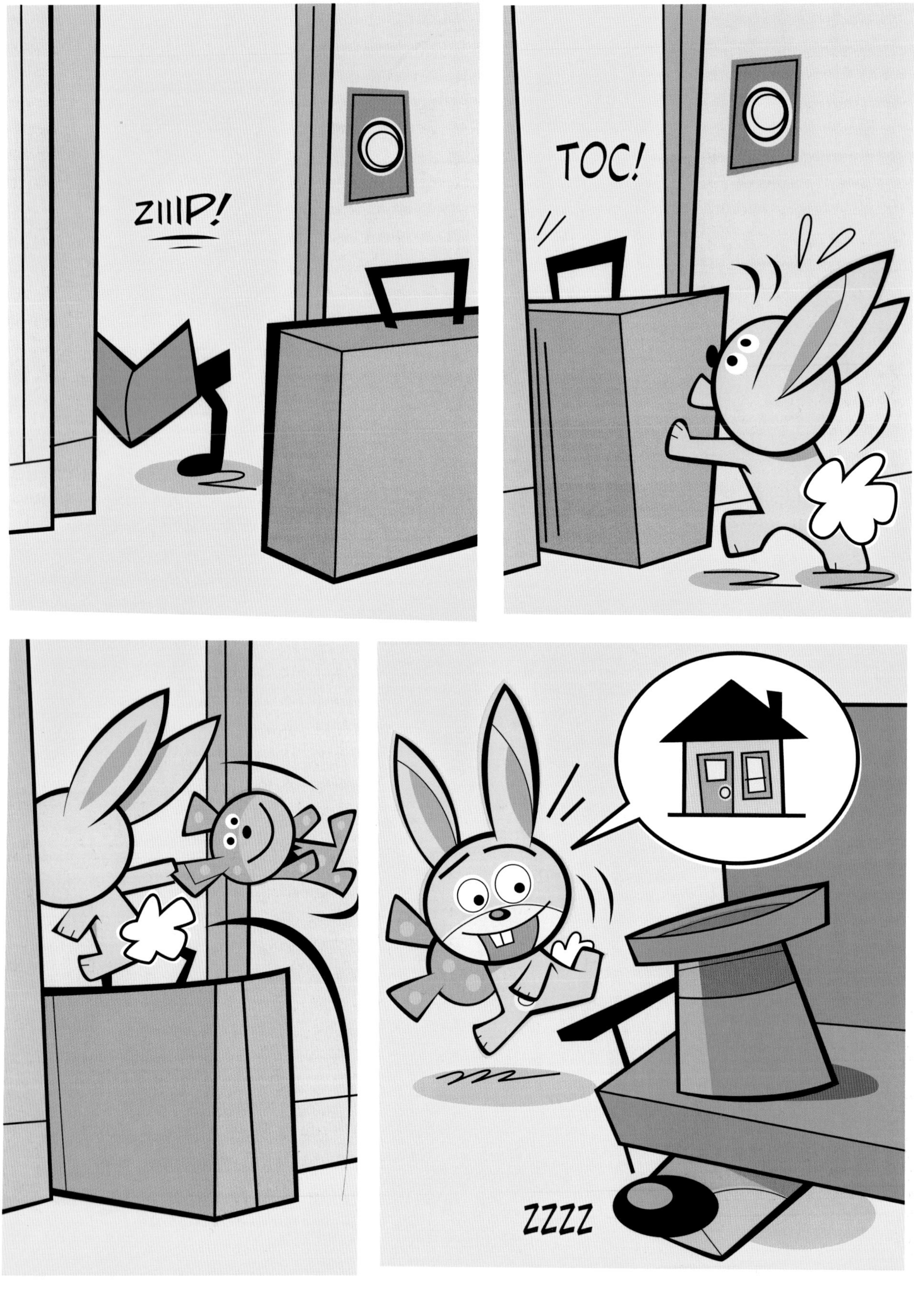
ZIIIP!
TOC!
ZZZZ

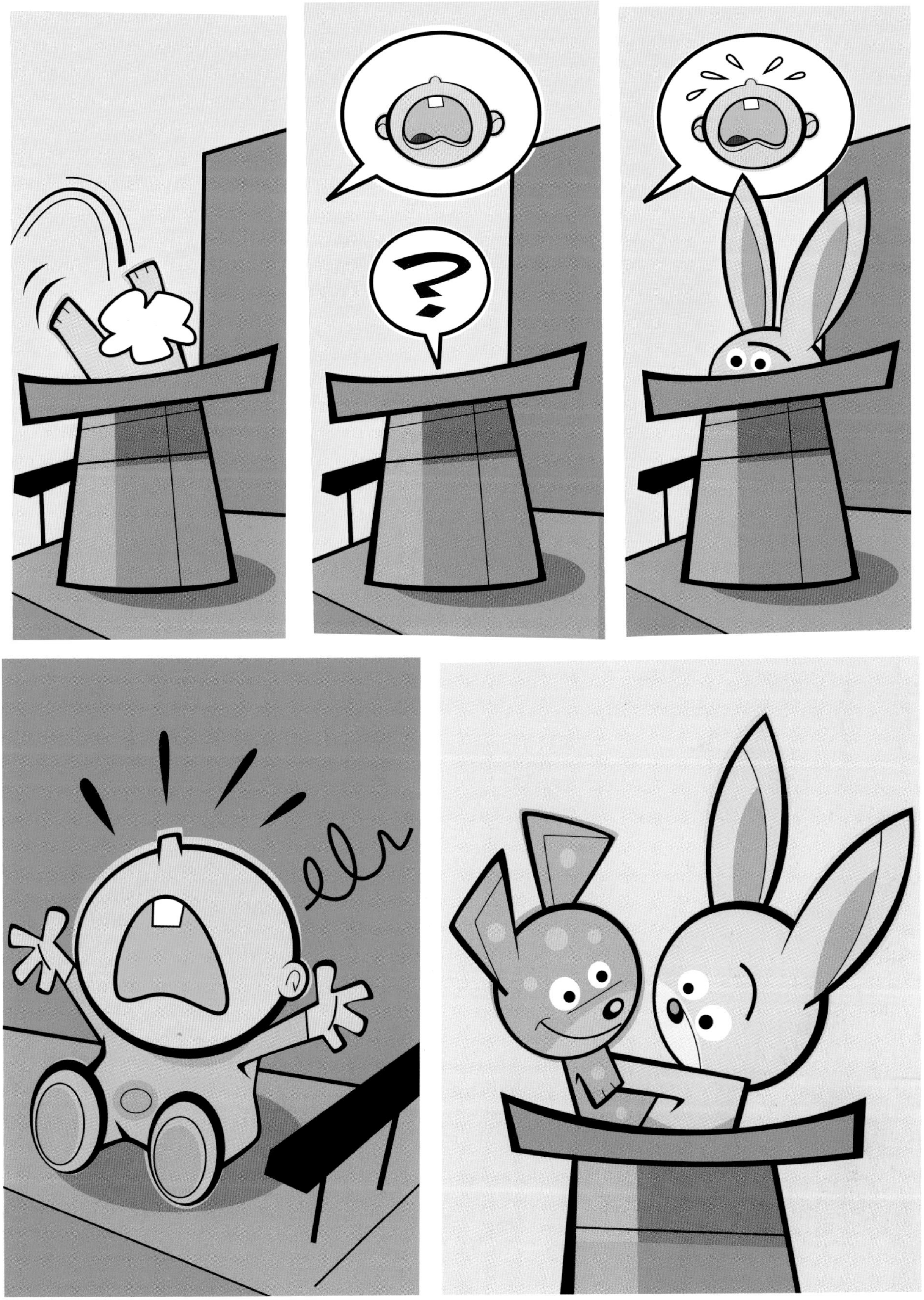

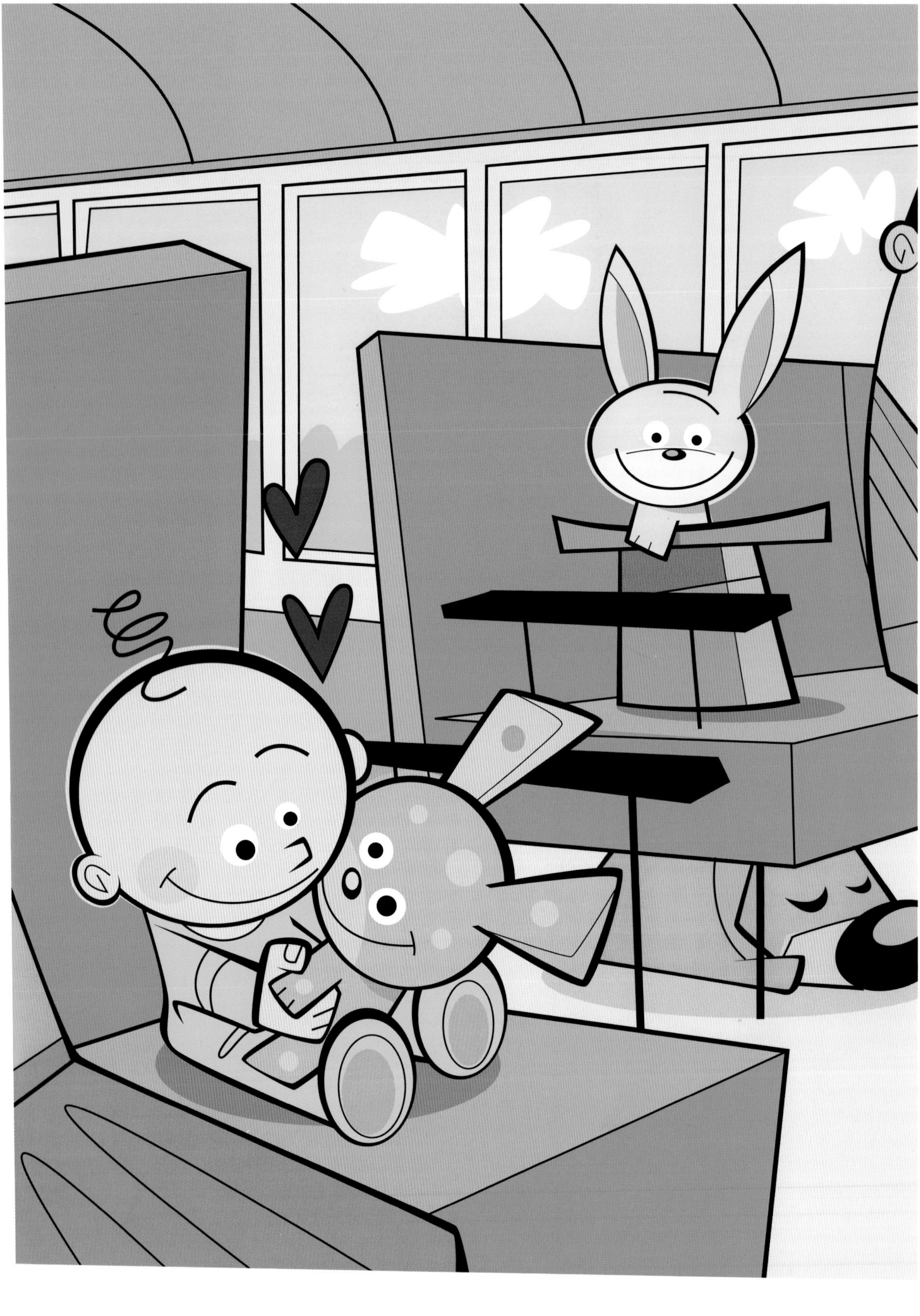